'TIL

FEAR

DO US PART

A GRIM AWAKENING NOVEL

BOOK ONE

MICHELLE GROSS

'TIL
FEAR
DO US PART

ISBN: 9781520155319

Table of Contents

'TIL FEAR DO US PART 1

    PROLOGUE 5

    CHAPTER ONE 12

    CHAPTER TWO 32

    CHAPTER THREE 51

    CHAPTER FOUR 70

    CHAPTER FIVE 96

    CHAPTER SIX 109

    CHAPTER SEVEN 118

    CHAPTER EIGHT 134

    CHAPTER NINE 169

    CHAPTER TEN 180

    CHAPTER ELEVEN 210

    CHAPTER TWELVE 247

    CHAPTER THIRTEEN 274

    CHAPTER FOURTEEN 286

    CHAPTER FIFTEEN 315

    CHAPTER SIXTEEN 346

    CHAPTER SEVENTEEN 359

    CHAPTER EIGHTEEN 399

    AUTHOR'S NOTE 407

Dedications
Without the constant support of my sister Tonya
and sister-in-law to be (one of these days), Nikki I
wouldn't be self-publishing the first book in the
series. You have no idea how much it helps
knowing you two love this series as much as I do.
All the nonstop talking about the characters and
ideas I put you both through while writing
Melanie's story on and off the past year, I'm
thankful for. All the help was extremely valuable
to my writing. The encouragement you both gave
me is what got me here.
And for all the readers: I hope you enjoy reading
Melanie's story as much as I enjoyed writing it.

PROLOGUE

How long does it take to change a person's life from happy to terrifying? How long was I normal before that part of me was taken away? How long would I live in fear after that?

I hummed quietly, chewing on my pen as I did a word search. I was short for my age so my feet swung out from my desk and occasionally hit Steven's seat—the boy that sat in front of me. He turned and gave one of those knock-it-off looks. I smiled, squinting my eyes together in apology and he turned back around.

"Okay, let's have recess outside today," Mrs. Wright told the class and excited glances were exchanged between everyone. They hurried from their seats and followed Mrs. Wright to the door.

"What are you doing? Hurry up Melanie!" Kimberly gestured with her hand for me to hurry, I smiled and stood up. My foot caught on something as I tried to walk. I looked down and saw that my shoelace was untied. I bent down to tie it. "Melanie!" Kimberly grew impatient.

"Go ahead, I'm coming." I didn't bother to look up. The room went quiet. I could hear their laughter trailing down the hallway.

By the time I had my shoe tied, I noticed the room seemed darker. As I stood, I caught sight of the windows in the classroom. Behind the alphabet curtains, it was pitch black. I tilted my head confused. Unease crept up my spine at the thought of bad weather. I never did like storms, but this darkness was unusual. I couldn't see anything outside. Something was wrong... How were they outside playing when it was so dark?

I needed to find my class. I started walking

toward the door when the lights started flickering. So, it was a storm? I was starting to get scared. I hurried to the door, but it slammed shut. Alarms went off in my head. How did the door shut when no one was around it? I stopped walking for a minute, looking around. The lights weren't flickering for now. I ran to the door deciding it was okay if I was freaking myself out as long as I got out of this creepy room by myself.

I grabbed the doorknob and twisted. It turned for me, but wouldn't open. I pulled hard against the door, it wouldn't budge. The lights started again. My mind always went back to the weather, but I heard no wind outside. No noise at all despite the rising sound of my breathing. I told myself to calm down. "Um, Mrs. Wright? Anybody? I'm stuck inside the classroom." I tried not to sound too afraid as I spoke through the door. I didn't want to look scared in front of my friends.

I turned around when the lights stopped flickering. The back row went out. My heart pounded and roared in my ears, my panic was becoming more than I could handle. Something told me this wasn't right. What was happening didn't make sense. Real fear was setting in. Another row of lights went out.

I started pounding my fists against the door. I yelled and screamed for someone to get me out of the room. I didn't know why no one could hear me. Something hissed in the room. I froze in place, hands still placed against the door. I went silent trying to listen for something in the room. Had I imagined it?

I studied the back of the room. Now that half the lights were out and the outside windows were dark, I couldn't make out anything beyond the darkness. My whole body went numb. I felt something in the room with me. I just knew...

I felt like I was being watched by something, a sickening presence. Pinpricks of fear broke out on my skin. The next row of lights went out. That left one more row before I would be in the dark. I studied the lights above me. *Please don't go out.* Why was this happening? It didn't make sense, yet... I squinted my eyes at the dark, it was closer. Too close.

"I found you." Never have I heard someone sound so sinister. It didn't sound human.

The last row went out. It was pitch black in the room. I couldn't make out my own hands. I brought my hands away from the door and covered my mouth. I felt my tears and knew I was crying, the sound echoed in the room. I felt something breathing in front of me. I froze, unable to move. I was paralyzed by my own fear. I couldn't even speak.

My feet were yanked from beneath me and the back of my head hit the floor. I lost my breath for a moment before trying to get back up. I didn't get a chance when something moved above me. That's when I found my voice. I screamed. I reached my hands out above me. I felt the presence trapping me. My hands touched something. A laugh that I will never forget erupted in the room. It wasn't a laugh; it was the sound of evil. My hand moved over what felt like a face. It latched onto my leg and pulled me closer. I flung my hands everywhere trying to protect myself. I hit something that was connected to its head and my panic grew. Did it have horns? I was going to die. I cried, tears running down my face. Why was this happening? How? I never realized I didn't believe in monsters until now.

Something scratched my chest twice. I cried out in pain. The pain turned to burning. My chest was on fire where it touched. It hurt so bad. I heard the turning of the doorknob in the distance. It released my leg and I felt the presence leave the room.

The next thing I knew the lights were turned on. A boy my age stood at the door. He looked shocked and ran to my side. He bent down next to me. "Are you okay?" he asked worried. I didn't recognize the boy, but I had never been so thankful for anyone. Before I could reply, the burning on my chest intensified. I grabbed my chest and cried out in pain. "What's wrong?" He panicked.

"My chest, it burns," I told him.

"Let me see." I didn't have time to think that he was a boy and I was a girl. We were only nine anyway. I let him pull down my shirt until we both saw what was causing me pain. A glowing red X seared my skin.

He touched it and flinched away unexpectedly, gripping his hand. "Ow." I stared at his hands as he held it out. The X drew itself onto his skin. The pain in my chest spread throughout my body. My vision grew dark until I lost sight of everything around me.

CHAPTER ONE

Nine years later...

Morning.

The word itself was ugly. I hated mornings. They were for happy, bubbly people who loved everything and everyone. I knew how to smile. Occasionally. I barely slept last night. Not that I sleep much any night.

I walked out the bathroom with a toothbrush wedged in my jaw and went to my brother's bedroom. "Alex, time to wake up." I flipped on the light and used my foot to kick his blanket onto the floor. He pretended to sleep. His eyes squinted as I walked closer, giving him away. The stream of sun coming from his window was in his face.

I sighed, "Get up. It's Friday then we're off

for two days." He continued to ignore me. I brushed my teeth for a second as I watched him. I smiled before kicking him off the bed.

"Will you stop? Gosh, you are so annoying." I grinned at his tantrum. There was something cute about seven-year-old brothers.

"Get up," I said through gurgles. I could barely speak with all the toothpaste in my mouth. I ran to the bathroom to spit it out. When I came back, he slammed the door in my face.

"You better be getting ready." I yelled through the door. I went to my room and got dressed. I slipped on a rock band t-shirt and worn jeans with a pair of old Nike's. I put my blonde hair in a ponytail and looked in the mirror. My blue eyes were big and bright compared to my pale skin. My pale skin always caused me to look sick, which probably had something to do with lack of sleep.

Oh, well...

Thirty minutes later, we left for school. I

always dropped Alex off at his elementary school. He was too much of a brat to ever ride the bus. "Is Mom off this weekend?" Alex asked, sounding hopeful.

I pulled in at his school. "Yeah, I think this was her last day for a few days." Our mom, Tina, was a nurse and worked night shifts so I took care of Alex a lot. Dad passed away a few years back.

"Good, I'm sick of your face," he mumbled as I pulled the Ford Focus to a stop in front of the school and he hurried out. He slammed the door before I got the chance to speak.

"Yeah, I love you too," I grumbled.

———————

Ryan Jones's big red Chevy was easy to spot in the parking lot. I smiled, knowing that meant Tess—his twin sister—was also here.

Thank goodness.

I hated walking around the school building alone. I had a way of catching people's attention. Not in a good way. More like I was the crazy girl.

I sighed getting out of the car. The letter 'C' in Campbell High School was missing above the entrance of the school building and the rest of the letters were faded and dirty looking. The school looked worse every year, and every year there was always rumors of the school shutting down. It never happened, which I was glad for. This was my senior year and I liked that it was small. The thought of going to Ridge High, a much bigger school and the next closest school, made me sick. It was three times as big as Campbell's, which meant too many more people and their need to question my sanity.

No, thank you.

Denver, Kentucky was a small town that only grew smaller. Decline of jobs and layoffs were destroying our region. Families were moving. It was slowly becoming a ghost town.

Speaking of ghosts...

I walked up the chipped steps that led to the entrance. To my right, several giggling girls walked through the grass next to the apple tree. There was a huge gust of wind that only ever blew there, and was currently blowing now. One of them wore a skirt and the wind picked it up revealing pink laced panties. She squealed all girly-like and held it down. Another one lost some papers she was carrying and ran to catch them while the others laughed, holding down their hair from the wind. A boy squatted behind them sneaking a peek at the one in the skirt. I rolled my eyes. His hair was permed and he dressed like he came from an eighties movie. His skin was sickly white and black circles framed his eyes. A blood stain covered a part of his blue shirt. I couldn't hide my annoyance when I watched him.

"This stupid wind," the skirt wearing girl grumbled. I didn't recognize any of them so they were probably freshmen. Poor girls, they were getting harassed by Fred. I was pretty sure that was his name since it was the name on the jacket he wore. Either that or he was wearing someone's jacket when he died. That was right.

Fred was dead. As in a ghost. *I'm Melanie Rose and I see dead people.* Did I forget to mention that?

Fred caught me staring and stood up. I shook my head and went inside. I searched the hallway for Tessa or Ryan. Everyone was still in the cafeteria besides a few loitering by the lockers. I went to my locker and grabbed the book I needed for my first class. I stared at the ugly green color of our lockers that needed an upgrade. Even the floors were cracking.

I closed my locker and turned around, feeling my eyes go all buggy as I jumped back surprised.

"Jesus, Ryan. Don't just pop up like that. I didn't even hear you," I warned him. He flashed a brilliant smile with equally perfect teeth. He was hot. He knew he was hot. The whole school knew. Sandy-brown hair and dark dreamy eyes. Of course, he was my best friend along with his twin sister.

"What's wrong? Did you think I was a ghost?" He smirked. He also knew how crazy I was. That I could see dead people. Or that I was delusional and messed up. I went through a lot of painful years of therapy in the past before realizing that I couldn't keep telling my parents that I saw them. So, as I got older, I started lying to the therapists and my parents until they were convinced that I was cured. Now the only ones that knew of my secret were Ryan and Tessa.

"Actually, yeah," I replied.

He scratched his chin as he leaned over me. I could smell the fresh scent of his aftershave. I inhaled deeply without meaning to. "So, is the couple lurking around today?" He was referring to the dead prom couple I told him about. They've been roaming the halls since we entered high school. I constantly caught them making out any and everywhere. I glanced over his shoulder and down the hallway then back toward the entrance.

"Not yet." That made him smile. I could never understand him. He never seemed bothered by the way I was. He stayed interested in everything I told him about ghosts.

"But I did see your sister and Mike disappear into the janitor's closet." I lied and grinned as his smile disappeared. He turned quickly, eyeing the janitors room. Mike was Tess's boyfriend for several months now.

I finally snickered. "Joking."

He turned back around. "Why you—" The bell sounded and students poured out of the cafeteria. The hallway crowded.

"Saved by the bell," I teased.

"There you are!" Tess grabbed my arm and pulled me away from her brother.

"What is it?"

"I'm mad at Mike." She shrugged her shoulders pulling me to first period. "I'll tell you about it later." I sighed, if only she wasn't mad at him every other day of the week.

I stared blankly holding my tray of nasty cafeteria food at Tess eating Mike's face off. Well, okay, they were making out, but it looked like they were eating each other. She didn't stay mad long. I never understood couples. I felt embarrassed just watching them kiss openly in the cafeteria. I'd never dated. Not that I wasn't asked, a few brave souls over the last few years found it in them to ask, despite the levels of weirdness I carried with me. It was like I was the broadcaster of weird.

I was more likely to end up with a dead boy at the rate I was going. I could taste the bitter jealousy in my mouth.

"Hey, Melanie." I turned to see Josh standing behind me. I looked nervously over his shoulder and felt the dread seep its way into my bones. Yes, she was always there. He looked over his shoulder trying to figure out what I was staring at. He frowned, confused. "You're always jumpy," he added with a smile. He was cute and sweet, but he wasn't the problem. He had a dead ancestor following him around.

She was a crazy old hag too.

"Oh... Yeah," I stammered, avoiding eye contact with the dead. His great-great-great—I don't know how many greats—grandmother glared at me. She placed her hands on her hips and tipped her nose up.

"Your hips are too small. How do you plan to bear children when you are so skinny?" She always said that. She never had a good word for any girl Josh spoke to. I ignored her.

"Melanie?" Josh gave me a puzzled smile. It was hard to have a conversation with him. I could never focus on just him.

"What do you see in this one?" she huffed at Josh, but of course he couldn't hear her. I rolled my eyes and realized too late that Josh was looking at me. This was why people thought I was weird. It was only going to get worse if I kept running in to ghosts like this one.

"Uh, my eyes are killing me." I tried to explain the eye roll. I needed away from these two. As sweet as Josh was, I couldn't handle his relative. "Bye!" I hurried off.

I caught Ryan staring, no doubt enjoying the view. He knew about the ancestor as well. He knew everything there was to know about my unfortunate life. Tess looked furious as she eyed me coming.

Uh-oh.

I took the seat next to Ryan. "Where's Mike?" I tried at a conversation to avoid her deadly glare.

She ignored me. "Melanie, Josh totally has the hots for you, but you always freak him out when you're in ghost-mode." I groaned. *Here it goes.*

"Chill, Tess. He has a dead grandmother hanging around." I gave Ryan the evil eye for that smartass comment.

"Ryan, please do not encourage this." She

motioned to him with her hands. "She needs to ignore the ghosts when people are around. That's why everyone thinks she's a weirdo. A freak." My evil eyes turned on the other twin.

"Easier said than done. You are not the one that sees them!" I hissed. Tess was gorgeous and perfect. Like her brother, she was both stunning and tall. Sandy-brown hair and dark eyes, bubbly and loud, everything I was not. And she's never seen a ghost unless it was in a movie. That was a plus.

"Have you ever thought that if you ignore them, they will naturally go away," she couldn't help but add. I shook my orange juice before opening it. Mike came back with two milks, handing one to Tess.

"Hey, Melanie," Mike managed to say.

"Hi," I muttered, stabbing my pizza with a fork. Mike looked afraid of me. Good lord, I was only making it worse.

"What did that pizza ever do to you?" Ryan

took the fork from my hand.

"So, movies tomorrow?" Tess perked up as she gave Mike dreamy eyes.

"Anything you want," was his answer.

Vomit.

"Melanie, are you coming too?" she asked and Mike went pale. Clearly, that was a nightmare itself if I was to join them.

"No, movies aren't really my thing." I had never seen a ghost at the theater before but hated running into unfamiliar ones. They tend to pop up out of nowhere and some could be very frightening. Besides, Mike looked like he didn't want me to go. Painfully obvious, I'd add.

"Yea, Melanie, let's go. How about a scary movie?" Ryan eyebrows shot up in a menacing way. God, he was evil. He was harder to deal with than ghosts sometimes.

"That sounds great!" Tess was already excited.

"I don't really like scary movies," I replied

curtly toward Ryan. He already knew that.

"Don't worry, you can hold on to me." I tried to ignore the flutter I felt in my stomach at his words. Ryan was my friend. Sure, he was a flirt, but he was like that toward every girl. I didn't know why he bothered with me. He was a good guy, though and a great friend. One that I would never risked losing over something as silly as romance.

The rest of the day went by slowly. I saw the prom couple in the hallway after lunch making out against someone's locker. I wondered if they even felt anything with them being dead and all. I didn't even know what it felt like to be kissed. I lived a rather pathetic life. People were afraid of me and the only boy who wasn't was off limits.

I was happy when the final bell sounded. I was one of the first ones out of the classroom. I crammed my books in my locker. That was the good thing about being a senior, hardly ever did I get homework. But now there was the rest of my life that I had to start figuring out.

My life goal? To stop seeing the dead.

Never going to happen.

Tess was outside saying bye to Mike when I walked out. Someone bumped in to me from the left. I tilted my head. "Oops." Haley held her hand over her mouth. I glared back. "Oh, it's just you." She dropped her hand to her side. "Freak." Her friends laughed with her and continued walking to their cars. I closed my eyes a moment and sighed. I hated them.

"They are so mean." Tess gave them the evil eye from behind.

"But it's not like what they said isn't true," I muttered as we walked together. It was my fault that so many people treated me like Haley did. They saw me talking to ghosts enough times time to think I was a freak. Stupid ghosts...

Why me?

"I don't care how many ghosts you see; I

still heart you." She swung her arm around me.

I smiled. "Yeah, screw everyone else. At least I have you," I added. She nodded in agreement.

"And my brother." My smile disappeared when the fluttering in my chest began. Sometimes it was easy to think of Ryan as a friend. Other times, I just wanted to kiss the crap out of him and figure out why all couples did it. My mind and heart were always in turmoil. *He is off limits, Melanie.*

"Yeah."

"Why don't you two admit that you like each other already?" Tess caught me off guard with her question. I stared, mouth gaped open.

"What? We don't--"

"Don't you lie to me Melanie Rose. I know where you sleep at night."

I looked to the ground as we walked. "You make it sound so easy."

"Because it is," she answered

"Not when you're me. Tess, you two are the only ones that accept me knowing everything. I can't even risk that just because I wished your brother would walk around without a shirt, twenty-four/seven." I spent our high school years watching the boys practice football so that I could catch Ryan with his shirt off. No, I wasn't that horny. Mostly. He was just that good looking.

"Yes you can." She laughed. "And ewe."

"No, I can't." I stopped at my car and grabbed the keys from my pocket.

"Can't what?" Ryan asked from somewhere behind me. I whirled around dropping my keys like I was caught saying something I shouldn't. I picked the keys up and looked at Tess. My eyes told her she better keep her mouth shut.

"Nothing," I told him.

"I'll call you tomorrow and let you know when to be ready," Ryan said.

"Huh?" was all I thought to say.

"Movies, remember?" Tess grinned. "We

are going to the movies. It's a *double date*." I was going to kill her.

"Tess, you guys need to go alone for it to be a date. Why do we need to tag along?" I grumbled.

"It's a double date. We gotta go." Ryan jingled his keys in his pocket looking bored.

"All right, see ya tomorrow Melanie," Tess chirped.

They walked to Ryan's truck and climbed in. Just like that, those two always did what they wanted. I smiled as I got in my car and drove home.

Mom had spaghetti and garlic bread made for dinner. Alex's attitude was so obnoxious, but I knew he was happy that Mom was off work for a few days. I disappeared to my room after eating.

Movies, really?

Dread settled in my stomach. I hated going out. I guess that made me a hermit. It was not that I didn't want to be normal. Live a normal life, get a boyfriend. *Not be a hermit.* Go shopping with

Tess. It just wasn't easy seeing new ghosts.

I heard sirens outside. I got off my bed and ran to the window. An ambulance was parked next door. It was Janet's house. She was an elderly woman. Was she okay? I watched several minutes from my window as two men went in and came out hauling Janet's small body on a stretcher.

I felt sick, my stomach knotting as I watched. I couldn't see too clearly since her driveway was partially hidden by a huge tree in the yard. I squinted trying to look through the branches. Then I saw it slip into the ambulance as they drove off. I stepped away from the window quickly, tripping over my foot in the process and fell backwards.

Alex came running through the door as I picked myself up off the floor. "Ambulance just came and got Janet that lives next door," he squeaked.

"Yeah, I know," I muttered.

"I hope she's okay. Mom's probably going to

go check on her at the hospital since she has nobody else." My heart sunk at his words.

I dropped down on the bed. I couldn't tell Mom that it would be pointless to go. It was already too late for Janet. She had to be dead. I was positive, because the cloaked figure that went through the ambulance as they sped off was the same thing that was standing over Dad's lifeless body in the hospital bed the moment he took his last breath.

CHAPTER TWO

Janet died last night. Mom returned not long after she left and told us what I already knew. I went straight to my room at that point, no use dwelling over it. People died, the world continued. With my lamp on, I tried to sleep but couldn't. When I did, I dreamed of the cloaked figure. I wasn't sure what it was, but I knew it wasn't a ghost. I'd only seen it twice. Last night and the morning my dad had died.

After a few hours of sleep off and on, I climbed out of bed around seven. With the sun spilling out through my window, I was comfortable enough to turn off my shade lamp that sat on my nightstand. I never, ever slept in the dark. I hated it. No, I was afraid of it. I never got over the horror I experienced being locked in a classroom when I was nine. What happened that day changed my life forever. After that, I started seeing the ghosts. I was young and traumatized. I could still remember the way I felt when I first saw one.

I tried to tell my parents like any child would do. It didn't go well. They didn't believe me and when I continued acting out because of it, it made things worse. After years in therapy, it caused a strain on my relationship with my dad, Steven. He became frustrated with his daughter who always claimed she saw ghosts. He thought I was making it up or maybe he thought I was losing my mind; I was never sure.

At thirteen, my parents were at their breaking point and was considering shipping me off to some crazy place. I decided right then that I had to pretend. Pretend that I was normal and could not see them. I had to fake my entire life and lie. I hated my parents that day.

It was easy after that; my parents were happy. More than happy, Alex was close to turning three and I was almost normal. I still acted strange at times when I saw a ghost, but I kept what I saw to myself. I guess they could handle that much. It was just a couple years later when Dad found out he had stomach cancer and died eight short months after. I was glad that I was on good terms with him before he passed.

The only person who believed me growing up was the same boy who turned on the lights in the classroom nine years ago.

Ryan.

I tried to ignore the feeling in my chest I got from the mere thought of him.

I slipped off my clothes and sat down in a hot tub of water. I sighed from the warmth that wrapped around my naked body. I looked down at my chest in a haze caused by the hot water sapping away my energy. Right above my left breast, there was the X that appeared the day I was attacked.

Ryan also shared the same mark on the inside of his palm from touching it when it was scorching my skin. We shared the same hideous reminder of the fear I'm most afraid of.

I scooted down further in the tub and closed my eyes. That was probably the reason he believed me. In a way, he experienced a little of whatever happened to me that day. I still didn't know what happened. I hated even thinking about it, but my mind always went back to that moment in the past. That was also the reason I could never ruin my relationship with Ryan. I could do away with any romantic feelings I have of him if that meant I could always keep him in my life. He was always there for me when my parents weren't. He still was. That meant a lot to a girl who saw ghosts.

So, no matter how sweet or sexy he was. Or how much I liked looking at him without a shirt or how good his butt looked in jeans, he was no longer the little boy that always held my hand when I was afraid. Now he was something dangerous to my heart, but that was all he will ever be. The boy I needed. I was starting to burn up. I'd better get out before I passed out from the heat. It also wasn't good for my heart or body conjuring up anymore images of Ryan. I needed to keep my feelings in check. I grabbed a towel and began to pat myself dry when the light flickered. My heart hammered in my chest. I told myself to stay calm and take a deep breath. The light could be about to blow. I was only imagining the worst because I had been thinking of the past. The flickering stopped and I waited. I tightened my hand over the towel. I slowly moved out of the tub and wrapped it around my body. The lights went out as my foot touched the mat outside the tub. I froze.

My chest heated up. I grabbed the X as it glowed against my skin, scorching me. The crimson red glow shined bright in the darkness. My stomach knotted with dread. No, please not again. I dropped the towel and ran for the door.

"Melanie." The voice whispered from

somewhere in the room. I could never forget the sound of pure malice. I fumbled with the door and screamed.

The light came back on. I was alone, naked, clinging to the doorknob. The room was empty. It was as if it didn't happen. I scanned the bathroom over and over. Nothing. I noticed something on the mirror and all the fear came back. I covered my mouth in horror.

You're Mine

I took the towel I dropped on the floor and wiped off the mirror. I put my clothes on and ran downstairs. It was around noon and Mom was sitting in the living room reading a book. She glanced at me, worry replaced her smile. "Melanie?"

I ignored her and looked outside. It was daylight. Mom was right here. I was okay. My hands shook so hard I squeezed them together so that she wouldn't see. It was happening again. I heard her move from the couch and felt her presence next to me. Only I didn't want to look at her. I knew what I'd see. I tried to swallow the foul taste in my mouth but I couldn't. "Honey, what's wrong?" She reached for me and I faked a smile and moved away. My brain tried to scramble for an explanation. What else was out there besides ghosts? What happened? Or was I really crazy?

"Nothing." I glanced away from the window. I could already feel her questioning my every move. "I thought I heard the phone ring while I was in the bath." I lied.

"No." I could feel the tension ease in her voice. Good, she was less worried about my sanity.

The phone rung and scared the crap out of me. I caught Mom's gaze analyzing my every move as I grabbed the phone. "Hello?"

"Hey." It was Ryan. My smile came natural.

"Ryan." I could hear the relief in my voice knowing that it was him.

"Is everything okay?" His question caught me off guard. Why was he checking on me?

"Yeah," I answered halfheartedly.

"Really, I thought...," he hesitated then sighed. "Never mind." He was acting strange. Why did he call? The burning of the X, did he feel it? I shook my head, that wasn't possible.

I heard Tess over the phone. "Give me the phone!" she yelled. I heard rustling in the phone, as if they were fighting over it. I pictured the two of them wrestling over the phone and grinned.

"Will you just go away?" he told his sister.

"What does she want?" I laughed.

"Who knows," he grumbled. "Fine, just for a second." I heard him hand the phone to her.

"Melanie, be ready at five," she ordered me.

"I could have told her that," Ryan argued in the background.

"She's my best friend."

"She was mine first," he added back.

"Yours?" I could hear the teasing in her voice and blushed. I was an idiot.

"Tess," I warned. "I'll be ready."

"All right, I'll let ya go."

"Bye."

The phone disconnected and I tried to ignore Moms piercing gaze and headed back to my room. "Melanie."

Ah, man.

"Yeah, Mom?"

"Where are you going?"

"Movies with Ryan and Tess later."

"Oh." She liked my answer. "Just you three?"

"No, Tess's boyfriend is coming."

"A double-date?" I saw the sparkle in her eyes. She loved Ryan.

"I wouldn't say that..."

"Ryan's grown into a nice looking young man," she added.

"Yeah, he's great," I told her and practically fled back upstairs.

————————

A few hours later, after eating several slices

of pizza, we were standing in line at the movie theater to buy our tickets. Unlike most of our town, the theater was in great shape. It was one of the nicer things in Denver. It made enough money off teenagers and couples to look halfway decent. Although I didn't agree with the spiraled-maze carpet. It made me dizzy looking down.

"Let's watch that one." Mike pointed toward the creepy looking poster.

"Yeah, that one looks good," Tess agreed. I didn't care so I let them decide, but it was getting harder and harder to ignore the ghost standing in front of us. He stood staring at the movie posters. I bit my lip nervously. The couple in front of us kept walking through him. "I'm freezing." The girl grabbed her bare arms. Her boyfriend smiled and began to rub them. If only they knew...

"I know that look," Ryan said beside me. I shrugged my shoulders. "Where is it?" he asked, interested. I pointed my head to the couple in front of Mike and Tess.

"He's staring at the posters," I told him.

"Is he picking out a movie?" Ryan teased but I only shrugged my shoulders again. I had no idea how ghosts lived or thought, but after years of watching them I would guess that he really might be about to watch a movie. They were unpredictable. The line moved forward. Tess followed the line and walked toward the ghost. People walked through ghosts all the time, but not without complaining of chills or headaches. I couldn't stand still and let her go through him. I reached out for her arm. "Wait, Tess."

She gave me a puzzled look. I had no way of explaining my actions. She hated me acting weird in public, especially if Mike was around.

"Um," I stammered. The ghost finally walked off. I smiled in relief. "Nothing."

It didn't take long for the line to move and we were buying our tickets and getting popcorn. Ryan bought everything for me despite my best efforts to tell him this wasn't a date. He simply ignored me. "What else do you want?" he asked smugly after telling the female worker we wanted a large popcorn.

I eyed everything and smiled. Okay, if he insisted. "A large coke for the popcorn. And some sour patches. Oh, and whatever those are!" I pointed to the chocolate looking candy on the counter. "Maybe some Reese's too?" He smiled pulling out his wallet.

The worker got everything I asked for. "What about your drink?" I added.

"We can share yours," he said without hesitation while I was losing all my composure. I looked at my flips-flops and concentrated on anything but him. I should have repainted my toes. The red polish was beginning to chip.

"You coming?"

We picked a seat in the back row. *I know*, how typical. Tess and I sat in the middle. Ryan sat at the edge of the row beside me. I loaded my popcorn down with salt and butter and it smelled so good. I positioned the popcorn between my legs and got comfortable. I grabbed a handful and started cramming it in my mouth.

"The movies not even started yet. And would you share those." Ryan leaned over and put his hand between my legs. Correction. He was reaching for the popcorn between my legs, but my breath caught and my mind went to indecent thoughts. He noticed that I stiffened and flashed his teeth. For once I was glad it was dark to hide the insane amount of blushing on my face and neck.

I grunted and moved the popcorn between us. That only made his grin bigger. I turned to Tess and caught her watching us. She smiled, knowingly. Well, she thought she knew something, but I was not going to let that happen. Ryan's slurping on *our* Coke caught my attention. He was staring at the blank screen. Seriously, he needed to stop.

What was wrong with me?

I wanted to fan my face but didn't. I needed to stop reading so many smutty books. It was obviously doing something to my virgin brain. Especially when he was around.

The small amount of lights that were in the huge room began to dim until it was completely dark. The screen lit up with previews. Ah, finally. I leaned back into the seat. Something needed to take my mind out of the gutter.

Fifteen minutes into the movie and I caught Ryan sliding his hand over my seat. He leaned closer to me, slowly slipping his arm around my neck. Wasn't that the oldest move in the book? I snuck a glance at him while he was looking at the screen. He was going to ruin my plan and our friendship if he kept on.

I looked to the screen again and squinted my eyes. That was strange. I thought I saw some sort of movement at the bottom of the screen toward the front of the room. I leaned forward so that I could see better. There was definitely something at the bottom of the screen. It started out as a tiny shadow that kept growing until it shaped into something monstrous looking. Was that fur?

No, not fur.

Unease settled in the pit of my stomach as it started to move away from the front and into the aisle. A shiver ran up my spine. Twice in one day? Just what was happening around me? That wasn't a ghost. It moved like fog and the shape was massive, but as it moved closer all it looked like was a black cloud. Of course, I was the only one that seemed to notice the thing. As it traveled up the aisle, a part of it expanded off, forming a hand. It was reaching out in my direction. There was no mistake, whatever it was, it was after me.

I needed to get out of here. My gut told me to run. The fog pushed through the seats and people. Their heads dropped in their laps as it passed over them. What? No one in the theater was paying attention to anything but the screen, a scary part was playing. Only I could see the one happening right in front of us. I jumped up hitting my knee into the seat in front of me. I moved over Ryan's long legs to get to the aisle.

"What the hell?" the girl that sat in the seat I bumped yelled.

I looked back for a split second. "Sorry." I ran out, the light in the hallway giving me comfort. I looked back and the blackness was oozing out the bottom of the doorway where I came from. I dodged angry people in the hall that glared or yelled at me running. I went for the bathroom; it was brighter than most places. I went to a stall and hid. I slammed my behind on the toilet seat and placed my feet up, cradling my knees. I tried to catch my breath and calm down. It seemed to help with every second I waited for the blackness to come and it didn't.

Just what was happening? What was I experiencing? Seeing ghosts, I somehow managed all these years. Scary fog that was after me was more than I could handle.

The black fog began pouring into the bathroom, up the walls, across the floor. I looked up in horror as the fog surrounded me, spreading, closing in. I wished that I was crazy. A tear slid down my cheek. I never knew what was happening or when the madness would ever end. The fog began to drop from the ceiling above me, making a hand. It reached for me. "Melanie." it slithered in hundreds of tiny voices. I leaned back as far as the toilet would allow me. The fog was on the ground—climbing the toilet.

The entrance to the woman's bathroom slammed open. Loud footsteps echoed through the room. The fog literally began to scream as the footsteps grew closer, each step evaporated the fog until it screamed itself out of existence. A pair of huge black boots stopped in front of the stall I was in. I quietened my whimpering when I realized I was doing it. One last bit of fog tried scrambling away from the boots, one raised to squash it. A tiny scream came from it as it sizzled until nothing remained. I froze when the boots pointed in the direction of the stall I was in.

Seconds felt like minutes as I waited for the mysterious person to open the door. I leaned to the side trying to catch a glimpse of whoever was on the other side. It was a man. Why was he in the girl's bathroom? He was covered head to toe in black. I couldn't see his face through the tiny crack but he was tall. *Really tall* and built if the boots were any indication of how big the man was. If he were some sort of attacker, I could never get away from him. I waited for my stall to be opened, waiting for my doom. Only, he turned around and left the bathroom. I heard the door shut.

I dropped my feet from the toilet and opened the stall. Nobody was in here. The black fog was gone. When I stepped out of the bathroom, Ryan was waiting. "What happened? You scared me back there." He looked worried but I couldn't make myself care at the moment. I was in danger. That was all that I knew.

"I need to go home," I stated.

He studied me a second before replying, "Okay, I'll take you home. Let me text Tess that we are leaving." He pulled out his phone and left his sister a text.

The ride home I barely said a word. Ryan wouldn't push for answers even if he knew something was wrong. When it came to my issues, he was more than understanding. Which made my heart ache, but this was even more than I can take. I had no idea what I saw but it wasn't good. I couldn't tell him.

So, I stared out the window into the dark of the night.

CHAPTER THREE

I didn't think it was possible, but the dark circles under my eyes were getting worse. That was bound to happen when a person never slept. I was on my third and last cup of coffee when Mom woke up at eight. An hour later Alex woke.

Sunday dragged by and I caught myself falling asleep on the couch around noon. The phone rung and I jumped myself awake. Alex was playing on Mom's iPad when it happened and shook his head at me before continuing whatever he was doing. I dragged myself off the couch and answered the phone by the third ring. "Hello?" My voice was a little hoarse from being so tired.

"You okay?" It was Tess. Her usual spunk was gone and replaced with worry I sensed over the phone.

"Yeah."

"What happened yesterday? Ryan said you sort of freaked out." I sighed through the phone, pinching the bridge of my nose. "You left not even twenty minutes into the movie. It had me worried. I'm sorry, was it the movie? I shouldn't have made you watch the scary one."

"No, it wasn't the movie." Although I wished it was.

"Then," she hesitated, "was it a ghost?" she whispered. I wanted to crack a smile that she was being so considerate of my secret.

Alex bumped into me on purpose as he ran to the kitchen. I glared as he disappeared through the hallway. I heard noise outside. "Did someone pull up?" I mumbled to myself. I went to the window and peeked out the blinds. Ryan's truck was in the driveway. What was he doing here? "Your brother just pulled up," I told Tess over the phone.

"Oh?" There was a twinkle in her voice that

was suspicious. I looked down at what I was wearing.

"Crap. I'm still wearing what I slept in." Black spaghetti strap shirt and pajama pants. She laughed over the phone. Oh, well. Before I went all girly, I knew it was for the best. He needed to see how unflattering I was. Like I wasn't enough on a daily basis.

I went to the door and opened it. Tess and Ryan were walking up the steps to the front porch. I glared at them as I hung up the phone. That was when I noticed the cake in his hands.

"Look at her." Ryan laughed. "She totally forgot."

"Totally," Tess agreed, and I sensed that they were making fun of me.

"What?" I paused and looked down at the date on the phone. September 18th. It was my birthday. Holy crap. I forgot my eighteenth birthday. How lame. I felt the blush on my cheeks. The torture of having pale skin. "Ugh." I tried to hide my embarrassment.

"Surprise." Tess hugged me. I stood there awkwardly. Ryan was grinning at me like a fool. A good-looking fool.

"Ryan, hurry with the cake before it melts." Mom walked to the door and ushered us in. I gave her a skeptic look. She knew they were coming over. Wait, I turned back to Ryan who held the cake.

"Ice cream cake." I perked up, eyeing the cake in his hand with renewed interest. Ice cream cake was the best.

"Now she's interested," he said. He was the last to enter and Mom shut the door behind him. He slipped off his Puma's and followed Mom into the kitchen. Of course, I followed after him. He did have the cake after all.

"Aren't I a little too old for cake?" I told them but my eyes never left the cake. Ryan sat it on the counter.

"You're a loser, anyway." Alex was sitting on

one of the bar stools.

"Alex," Mom warned him. I sighed at the sad truth my brother spoke. Even he knew what a loser I was. Stupid ghosts, thanks for ruining my life.

"There's my Alex." Tess gave him a dazzling smile and his whole face turned red. He couldn't deny he was my brother in that category. We both blushed like idiots. He had a thing for Tess.

"Shut up," he told her then looked at me. "How does someone forget their birthday?"

"Now, now," Tess continued to pester him.

"Happy birthday, Melanie." Ryan loomed over me, smiling bright.

"Thanks."

"Happy Birthday!" Tess attacked me from the side with a hug.

"Can we cut the cake already?" I grumbled.

—————

An hour later, I was on the back porch sitting. It was nice and pretty; weather was just right. I stared blankly at the old tire swing in our backyard. Tess and Ryan spent many summers back here with me swinging each other on that thing. I smiled. It was easier some days more than others. Some days, like today, I was okay. I stayed home and never saw any ghosts. I could imagine I was normal.

But I would never live a normal life.

I knew my life was heading nowhere. I wanted to be stronger, really. The thought of spending every birthday with Mom sounded... sad. I loved her, but people my age were out doing things they shouldn't with friends. I even held back Tess and Ryan.

"Hey." Tess grabbed the seat next to me and sat down.

"Where's Ryan?" I asked.

"Helping your mom do something. I don't know," she mumbled and I smiled. He was sweet. My smile disappeared as quickly as it appeared. It was wrong to want him to stay with me.

"You seem even more down than you normally are." She studied me with a sad smile on her lips. "And I didn't think that was possible."

"I just want to be normal," I gave her the truth.

"I like you the way you are," she replied. That made me smile for a split second.

"I don't understand you and Ryan. Why are you even my friend?" I stood up, not wanting to get emotional but knew I already was. Yesterday messed with my head. "My own parents never believed me, but you two," I grabbed my chest, "I'm sorry."

"I have no idea where this is coming from, but could you please stop?" she sighed. "I don't know what's going on and I know there's no way for me to understand but I don't need to. I accept what you see that I don't. I don't need an explanation because sometimes things can't be explained." I stared at her. "Okay, enough. These sorts of conversations make me want to vomit. So, whatever you see, that's cool. The day you and Ryan told me your secret, I laughed but I believed you. For some strange reason." She stood while scratching her jaw and walked over to me. "You see ghosts, whether it's real or in your head. We still love you regardless." As horrible as that last part sounded, she had me feeling better.

I laughed. "I could kiss you right now."

"Well, don't. I'm not into that sorta' thang and my brother just might kill me if I did." I laughed harder.

"Thanks, I needed that."

"That's what I'm here for."

"What are you here for?" Ryan opened the screen door and stepped on the porch.

"For Melanie. She's the birthday girl," she answered. I rolled my eyes.

"What a sad life." I bent my arms onto the porch railing and gazed into the distance.

"Hey, I got an idea." Ryan and I both groaned when Tess spoke.

"I'm not sure I wanna know," Ryan said, stepping close to me.

"Let's plan a party on the old strip job near Bernie's next weekend. Melanie never does anything exciting, and that needs to change. I'll invite a ton of people."

"I don't think so," I said quickly.

Ryan was quiet. I turned my head, the crease in his forehead told me he was considering the idea. "It does sound entertaining." I frowned at him.

"See, it will be fun. You've never been to one." She was getting excited now. I was trying to find a reason why I kept saying no. Other than my ghost problem, there were none. I needed to take back a part of my life the ghosts took from me and ignore the new one from last night.

"Will there be alcohol?" I wondered aloud.

Tess snickered nudging her brothers shoulder. "Will there be alcohol?" she mimicked my words. "Listen to how innocent she sounds."

"You don't have to drink if you don't want to," Ryan added. He was probably afraid that might scare me away from going. He was always looking out for me. I smiled.

"No, I think I will." I would. I was tired of my life. I needed something to keep my mind off what happened last night.

"Really?" Ryan looked surprised. Not as surprised as I felt. It was a pleasant sort of feeling though.

"Yes! I have been waiting for this day." Tess jumped.

––––––––

They were long gone when night fell and Mom went to work. Alex fell asleep on the couch. I debated on leaving him there but didn't. I turned off the cartoons he was watching before I picked him up. I barely made it up the stairs with him. He was growing so much these days, I barely had the strength to carry him. I remembered when he was way cuter than the brat he was now. My back felt huge relief when I dropped him on his bed. I stretched out the pain before I walked out of the room.

I was almost to my room when I heard the TV downstairs. I turned it off before I laid Alex down. I was sure. Well, pretty sure. I walked downstairs and turned it off. I left the small shade lamp on in the living room. I needed some sort of light on in the house in case I was to get up through the night. I made it to the stairs when the TV came back on.

I stopped moving. Hardly breathing, I tried to tell myself I was imagining it. I slowly turned back to see the light of the television casting a glow into the hallway where I was. I tried to tell myself not to panic. The knots in my stomach tightened. I walked back into the living room. I hurried to the coffee table, grabbed the remote, and hit the power button. I waited for something to happen, scanning the room. Nothing did. No ghosts. I thought of the fog from yesterday. It wouldn't come again... would it?

"Ah!" I pulled down my shirt to look at the X. It was glowing red, burning my flesh again. Something was about to happen. It all started every time this X heated up my skin. The pain grew stronger. I ran to the phone, but it wasn't at its base. I started to look around the room for it. The TV flickered on. Fear pumped through my veins.

I ran into the hallway toward the stairs, but stopped when I saw what stood at the top. A young girl wearing a yellow sundress with tiny white flowers. She looked a little older than Alex. Only she was dead. Her skin was sickly white as most ghosts were but that wasn't how I knew. A blotchy red stain covered the left side of her stomach. She wasn't a normal ghost... Her eyes burned red. I staggered backwards into Mom's bookshelf in the hallway. The curve of her mouth slid up in a sinister way as she tilted her head to the side. I was screwed.

She was holding one of her hands behind her

back. She began to move the arm tucked behind her, in her hand was a tiny thin sword, but it was just as big as her in height. She was going to kill me. She started down the stairs and I turned on my heels to run.

"There's no point." Her voice was that of a child's and she laughed, "Tonight, you die."

I ignored her. I wasn't going to wait for my death. I ran outside knowing she would follow. If this was how I was going to die; I wouldn't let anything happen to my brother. I doubted she wanted anything to do with him, though. They all seemed to want me.

I opened the front door and ran off the porch barefoot. I looked around our yard deciding where I should go. We lived at the end of the hollow up on a hill. My closest neighbor was at the bottom of the hill—besides Janet who passed away. I looked back into the house and saw the shadow of her tiny frame walking through the hallway. The grass was cold on my feet as I went for my car. I cried out when I realized it was locked. My keys were still in the house. She was already outside. I knew it was over, but that didn't mean I would give up.

Then things got stranger. A figure appeared in front of me. I fell back against the car causing my head to hit the window. I grabbed my head and shook the pain away. At the rate I was going, I was only helping them kill me. I looked up to whoever was before me. The guy was tall, that was the first thing I noticed about him. The second was the way his dark hair spiraled out of control. He didn't look like a ghost from behind. His clothing was black which probably wasn't a good sign. My eyes widened when I looked down and saw the boots. The same boots that were in the girls' bathroom last night. It had to the same guy!

I sat there stunned until I figured he wasn't going to turn around. I didn't know what he was doing. I took that as my chance to scoot away. I was so focused on him that I didn't notice that scary ghost girl had somehow ended up on the car.

The sword she held hovered above me. She lifted it over her head smiling at me.

Then everything happened at once. I tried to make a run for it but ran straight into his broad chest as the blade came down over us. The ghost girl only seemed to notice him at that moment, her evil smile turned to horror. She moved backward in an unnaturally way. "You!" she hissed at him before jumping off the other side of the car. His boots crunched as he strode around the car to where she jumped.

I started running. I didn't get past the third step before a strong arm wrapped around my waist and pulled me backward, into his chest. I panicked, kicking and thrashing. "Let me go!" I screamed.

"I can't do that." He replied and a shiver ran up my spine. What was he going to do to me? My heart pounded out of control. "Will you stop?" He took a deep breath. I felt his breath against my hair when he released it.

"Let me go," I said again. "I don't know

what you want but let me go!"

He let go while I was still fighting him and I fell onto the gravels. Rock buried into my knees from the unexpected fall. I ignored the sharp pain. "There, happy?" he grumbled. "I have other things to be doing *human.*" I was still on my knees, but I was too afraid to turn around. I could feel his gaze burning into my back. He sighed. "So, what do you plan to do when Molly comes back? Oh, believe me, she will be back. And many more."

I picked myself up and finally turned around. "Molly?" I finally got a look at his face. He was handsome, in an older, rugged way. His eyes were cold and dark. His hair was wild and unruly. I knew he was dangerous. Then I remembered what he said. "What do you mean, mere human?" He spoke as if he wasn't one.

His mouth curved up in a wicked way that made him look terrifying. "Molly is the one that just tried to kill you. Although, she is no girl."

"Yeah, thanks for stating the obvious," I

spat. He grinned and that somehow made him look even more lethal.

"You understand that much. You can see ghosts." It was not a question, he merely stated. Just who was he? "Let me put it this way, Melanie." He stepped closer. "There's a lot more than ghosts, things you never thought possible. This is only the beginning."

"What do you mean?" I frowned.

"What I'm saying, *human*, now that you're eighteen, you are nothing but a target to every demon in the Underworld." I stood there, mouth opened, trying not to burst into giggles at how ridiculous this guy sounded. Only I was afraid, he was scary. I couldn't laugh no matter how insane it sounded. Demons? Underworld? My life was messed up, maybe that's why I couldn't not believe what he was saying. "Most of all, a very evil and powerful entity is after you."

"What?" I muttered, barely managing to hear his voice through all the thoughts running through my head. He grabbed my shirt and yanked it down. He exposed the X above my left boob. Because of his barbarian action, I felt violated causing my hand to connect with his face. A loud smack echoed through the air, followed by the stinging on my hand.

His head jerked from the impact of my palm. It was only at that moment that I realized what I did. His expression darkened, an evil gleam pooled in his eyes.

"Very foolish," he warned me. I took a step away from him. "Not a very nice thing to do to the person that's here to keep you safe." He's here to keep me safe? I should be running away from him. Everything about him screamed danger.

"I don't even know you. Like I would believe anything you just said."

"Ah, you have a point." He moved his hand to his chin as he watched me. "But something tells me you already do. Soon enough, though, you will understand everything."

"Just stay away from me. Don't come here anymore!" I told him, walking away backwards so that I could keep an eye on him. I had my hands in front of me for protection. (As if that would stop him if he wanted to attack me.) He never followed me. My heels caught the porch and I fell back onto the steps.

Ow, my butt took the fall, but I refused to rub the ache.

"You're not even listening to a word I'm saying." A dark eyebrow rose in amusement.

I picked my throbbing butt off the steps and ran inside. I locked the door and peeked out the window but the stranger was already gone.

CHAPTER FOUR

"Ms. Rose, this is the third time I've woken you up. Stand up." My forehead hit the desk when she startled me awake. I winced, rubbing my forehead. Everyone laughed except me. I stood slowly using all the strength I had to stay awake. I was so tired. Even the thought of what happened last night couldn't keep me awake.

Mrs. Thorn glared through her overly big glasses. She expected me to stay awake when this class was so boring? All she ever did was talk and read books that either made me sad or bored me to death. It was beginning to sound like a lullaby. A horrible one. I didn't sleep last night. I was afraid to.

Lunch was no better. I barely had an appetite

but funny thing, most of my food was gone on my tray. I guess nothing could keep my appetite at bay, even lack of taste buds and ghosts trying to kill me. Or maybe I was hungrier than I realized? Or so tired that I never noticed all the food I was stuffing in my face.

"What is with you today?" Tess looked at me as if I was some science experiment gone wrong.

"I couldn't sleep." I didn't sleep. And I had no intentions on telling her why.

"Yeah, your dark circles gave that away. So, what's up? New ghost?" She leaned over so that no one could hear what she asked.

"I guess you could say that," I mumbled. Ghosts never tried to kill me before.

"Seriously, what is with ghosts? Don't they realize once you're dead, you're supposed to rest in peace. Not loiter around with the living," she grumbled. I agreed, but that didn't change the fact that some chose to stay. I always wondered why some wandered as a ghost. Was it unfinished business, regrets, or love? Whatever the reason, I wish I didn't have to see them. I would rather not know like everyone else and walk around completely ignorant. Because if you never saw them, they'd just be another scary movie.

"Where's Mike?" I noticed that he was missing from the table.

"Oh, the football team is eating together over there." She pointed to loud group of boys wearing jerseys. I spotted Ryan. That explained why they weren't with us. Some sort of pregame ritual, I guessed. "They have their first scrimmage game tonight and they're pretty pumped." I could tell from all the laughter and hollering among them.

"On a Monday?" I asked. Did they normally have games on Monday? I couldn't remember. Ryan noticed me staring from across the cafeteria. He smiled and my insides turned to mush. He walked toward us.

"Hey." It sounded more like a question than a greeting.

"Hey," I said back.

He blinked a few times, deciding on whether he should say what he wanted. He looked down at his feet before asking. "You coming to the scrimmage game tonight?"

"Ah," I mumbled.

"We will be there," Tess answered. And that was the end of that. I was going now whether I wanted or not. But it was never a bad thing seeing Ryan play. I loved to. The problem was I had no idea when something bad was going to happen again.

After school, I picked up Alex and took us home. I made steak and baked potatoes. Mom had just woke up when we got home. She staggered around the house still half asleep wearing her red robe and mismatched pink pajama bottoms. Night shift was rough on her, but it was what she preferred. We sat and ate together, it was like any other Monday.

I began to relax more by the time I arrived at the football field. I brought a thin jacket with me, the nights were beginning to get chilly. A sign summer was ending and autumn was taking its place. I always enjoyed the crisp smell of fall air.

After paying my way in, I found Tess hugging Mike next to the field. He was already wearing his padding underneath his jersey. I slipped through the metal fence made of three bars that separated the bleachers from the football field.

The bleachers were already filling up with people, which surprised me since it was just a scrimmage. But our small town loved local football and a lot were freshman and sophomores that weren't even interested in the game. They came to mingle and attract the opposite sex.

"Melanie." I turned to see Ryan running toward me. He looked so good in his jersey, with all the padding and tight white pants that would soon be stained with grass and dirt. He made the ugly green color of our school look nice.

"Hey." I beamed at him.

"Whoa, you're in a good mood." He grabbed his chest like he was stabbed. "Your smile caught me off guard. You're so beautiful when you smile."

That smile was because you are so nice to look at. "Thanks, Ryan. You make it sound like I'm a scrooge." I punched his arm playfully.

"You're the one that said it." I gaped my mouth open at his words and he laughed. My chest ached. Why couldn't he be a jerk? The whistle startled me and the coach began calling all the players in. Ryan looked to his coach then back to me. He leaned his cheek to my face and pointed a finger toward it. "A kiss for good luck." I wanted to do what he asked and that was what made it dangerous. I couldn't let myself act on my feelings, even if our feelings were the same. I turned my face away and nudged his cheek with my palm. He smiled like it was enough. "Was that for good luck?" he asked.

I couldn't speak so I simply nodded. We

stared at each other several moments before he ran to catch up with the others.

"It's sad watching you two dodge your feelings for one another." Tess was next to me without me realizing until she spoke. I glanced at her then to my feet. I had nothing to say. She was right. Ryan had gone out of his way all summer letting it be known that he wanted more than a friendship with me. But because of me, of the way I am, we were stuck as friends. I wouldn't drag him down to my world. "Let's go sit down," she said. Maybe she sensed I couldn't deny my feelings for him at the moment. So, we stayed quiet.

I grabbed the top bar of the fence and slipped back onto the other side when I noticed him sitting on the bleachers. It was impossible not to notice him. He looked out of place. He still wore dark clothing but his leather jacket was missing. A black t-shirt fit snugly against his muscular frame. His intimidating glare said don't-mess-with-me. Everyone seemed to go out of their way to avoid him. The bleachers around him were empty. He stretched out one of his legs covered in dark jeans that disappeared into his boots.

What was he doing here? Was he following me? As if he knew what I was thinking, his eyes met mine. He tilted his head as his gaze devoured me. I looked away. I got my answer, he was following me.

"Who the hell is that guy?" Tess asked in her usual loud voice. I panicked.

"Don't stare at him!" I warned her quickly, grabbing her arm. I looked down, around, anywhere but where he sat.

"What's wrong with you?" She arched her eyebrow. This was Tess I was talking to, I should have known not to tell her to do something. She would do the exact opposite. She snapped her head back to check him out, very thoroughly. Her eyes traveled his entire body. I was irritated with her; she couldn't see the danger. I hadn't told her anything, though so I had no right to be upset. "If you look over the broodiness about him, he's very attractive." I gave her a skeptical look. Nothing about him felt attractive to me. Scary? Yes!

"He looks dangerous," I pointed out.

She laughed and bent her body to go through the bars, I was already on the other side. "That makes him even more sexy."

I couldn't win an argument with her. It was better to drop the subject altogether. Tess wasn't one to let anything drop, though. I followed her to the bleachers, frowning when I realized where she was taking us. She took the seat right below him. She smiled and patted for me to join her. I wanted to tell her no, but that would only drive her to be more reckless. I glared at him as I sat down.

My back felt like it was on fire and I had a feeling he was still staring at me. I placed my jacket next to me and tried to concentrate on watching the boys warm up on the field. The opponent's bleachers were crowded as well.

I smiled when I found Ryan's jersey number,

twenty-three, on the field. "I see Mike," Tess said, pointing at him. I smirked thinking we were doing the same thing.

"I found Ryan," I added.

"Excuse me," a shy voice of a girl behind me said. I was curious, but not enough to turn around and risk making eye contact with him. Tess turned around to look though. "My friend wanted me to ask if you could tell us your name." Curiosity finally got the best of me and I turned around. Three girls hovered close to him, blushing and fawning over him. They looked to be about sixteen. Only he looked annoyed. He tilted his head, I saw the tick of his vein across his jaw as he glared at them.

Their smile faded. "Sorry," one said hurriedly.

"We just wanted your name." Another one grabbed the girl in front and begin to pull her away. "Let's go."

"What a jerk," she muttered before they all

walked off. He watched them leave then turned back to me. I was too slow at trying to turn away, I knew he caught me staring. Oh, now that he had, I guess there was no point in stopping. His eyes were cold and disapproving as they bore into mine.

He leaned forward, closing in on me. He placed his elbows on his knees and made a devilish smile that wasn't a smile at all. "Relax your expression, you look as if you want to rip my heart out." I tipped my lip up in disgust. He wasn't entirely far from my thoughts. Only I would choose to rip out those cold, calculating eyes of his first.

"Do you know him?" Tess studied him, the way he was so close to me.

"No," I said abruptly, but I knew it sounded like a lie.

"I was just at your house last night." He dropped the bomb, and Tess's pretty face wrinkled with surprise.

"Melanie?" She looked to me for an answer.

"I don't know who he is." I admitted.

"Not yet. But you will," his deep voice promised. Just what was he trying to do?

"Just ignore him. He's creepy," I replied, not caring that he heard me.

"I don't know..." she hesitated, tilting her eye while she stared at him. "Are you flirting with Melanie?" I opened my mouth to the horror that just spilled from her lips.

Before I could answer, he laughed bitterly. "No." He looked repulsed by the idea and now I was the one feeling offended. "I'm just speaking the truth."

"Let's go sit somewhere else." I grabbed my jacket as I stood up and walked away. I didn't look back to see if she followed. I hoped she would.

Seconds later and she was by my side. "That guy was strange," she mumbled.

"Creepy. Scary. Crazy," I added.

"Should we, maybe report him or something? He did say you'd get to know him.

That was scary." She turned back to where he sat. "He's still staring at you." She sighed. "And to think he's so good looking."

I groaned. "No, I don't want to report him, but I do think I should go home. Will you tell Ryan that I have a headache and went home?" I asked.

She smiled. "Yeah, of course. Do you want me to come with you?"

I shook my head. "No, stay and watch your boyfriend play." I grabbed her shoulders and squeezed, reassuring her I was okay. I wished I was.

"Okay, text me when you get home."

As I walked away from the bleachers and to the parking lot, I was constantly looking over my shoulder. I couldn't shake the feeling that he was following me. I felt some comfort as I made it to my car and got in. I was putting on my seatbelt when I noticed something in the rearview mirror. I looked back into the mirror and screamed. The ghost girl was in the backseat. I let go of the seatbelt and reached for the door. I heard the click of the doors locking. "Not going to get away this time." Her dark hair floated in the air as she threw herself between the front seats. I screamed for help and tried to open the door.

She pulled out a small knife or maybe it just appeared in her hand. I reached for her hands as she swung at my neck. My hands went through her, but I leaned back enough that her knife missed my neck and sliced my shoulder.

"Ah!" The pain tore through me.

Someone opened the back door. She lunged for me again, but her body was jerked out from the back door. She screamed a hideous sound that made me cover my ears. I reached for the door and this time it opened. I stepped out, holding my injured shoulder. It was him again and somehow; I wasn't surprised. He held the ghost by her neck. She wiggled and hissed in his grip. "You are quite brave Molly. Coming back for her, knowing I'd be here," he told her.

"She doesn't belong in this world any longer. She belongs to him!" She smiled as if she won before looking at me. "Her fate is sealed."

"I don't think so." He glared, tightening his grip around her neck. She laughed once more before vanishing. He swore before dropping his empty hand. I stayed still, seeing him there but feeling my mind elsewhere. I was trying to understand what the ghost had said.

"Hey," he called to me. When I didn't reply or look up to him, he shook me. "Hey." He sounded annoyed. That finally caused me to snap out of it. I shook my head and looked up. His hand was over mine as I held it over the nasty gash on my arm. "Let me see," he ordered.

"Huh?" I was still stunned.

He sighed. "Let me see your shoulder. How bad is it?" Oh, I moved my hand and saw all the blood on it. I was shaking and tried to calm myself. He didn't miss anything I tried to hide. He watched me close my bloodied hand before asking, "May

I?" I started tugging my t-shirt down off my shoulders and he helped. I wanted to cry out as we moved it over the wound. It was a nasty looking cut and deep. It was worse than I thought.

"How did a ghost do this?" I asked.

"She wasn't a ghost," he answered. "She was, but she became a poltergeist. She was given even more demonic powers after that."

"Demonic powers?" I tried to laugh but it sounded closer to a cry. So, I stopped altogether for the fear of crying.

"Don't ask things, Melanie. Not yet. Not until you're capable of understanding what's happening." His expression was hard and impossible to read. I needed to know who he was. How he saw what I saw and just what exactly he was himself. But more than anything, I wanted to know what was happening to me. He seemed to know. He looked behind him, I followed his gaze to vehicles pulling in the parking lot. A group of teenagers wandered around, not interested in the game, just wanting to hang out. "We should go somewhere more private."

He grabbed my hand, catching me off guard with how his fingers caught with mine. I stared at our hands together as he led me to the passenger seat of my car. He opened the door and tossed me inside. Really, he just shoved me in there. I studied my hand, knowing it wasn't a good idea to be letting a stranger do as he pleased with me. He held the answers I wanted, though. He moved around the front of the car and got in the driver's side.

"Where are you taking me?" I asked cautiously.

"Home," he answered. I hadn't expected that answer.

Ten minutes later, he was pulling the car into my driveway. I hadn't believed he was telling the truth until then. I unbuckled my seatbelt and glanced at him. Now why was this suddenly so awkward. I went from hating the guy, being afraid of him, thinking he was a liar... Just who was he?

A new understanding passed over me. I would just have to get to know him.

I wasn't sure what I was supposed to say to him as he turned off the car. "Um, thanks?" I offered.

He raised an eyebrow at my new-found manners before looking toward my house. "Go upstairs to your room."

"What?"

"I'll meet you up there." He placed his hand on the steering wheel.

"Wait a second—" I started to argue, but he cut me off with a single glare. Not sure I could do anything else, I did as he said. I went inside. Mom and Alex were watching a movie. I said a quick "hello" and hurried upstairs before either of them could see my shoulder. I closed my bedroom door behind me. When I turned back around, he was there.

"You're really in my room!" I hissed at him.

"Sit down." He must love ordering me around. When I didn't, he grabbed my arm and forced me to sit down on the bed. How did he get in my room? I eyed him suspiciously. I was too quick at getting up here for him to have found a way to climb.

He sat next to me, moving me closer as he tugged my t-shirt down. I winced from the pain. "Are you going to start freaking out?" he asked. I got nervous when he asked.

"It depends, why are you asking?"

"Don't freak out," he warned.

"Oh my god," I said now on the verge of freaking out. "What are you gonna do?" I willed myself not to panic. Too much.

He looked irritated. "Will you stop? You're doing exactly what I said not to." I tried to get up, but he pushed me back down on the bed.

"You shouldn't have told me not to freak out, that's only making me freak out," I heaved.

He arched a dark brow before sighing. He

gripped my arm while putting his free hand on my cut. Something warm hit my shoulder. I could see a white glow spreading underneath his palm. It heated my skin to the point that it was almost ticklish. The glowing stopped and he removed his hand. I stared in amazement at my shoulder. It was healed. No mark, scab, or scar to show that it had ever happened.

"Oh," I said in awe. "Oh." This time in horror. I looked up to him with fear. "What are you?"

"I wonder..." He avoided the question.

"Why is she trying to kill me?" I whispered. "And that thing at the movie theater, you stopped it from hurting me." When he looked away, I knew I was right. "Answer me."

"I already told you, demons are after you. One in particular has had his sights set on you a long time. How long have you had the mark on your chest?" he asked.

"Since I was nine. I was attacked by

something."

"It's been since then that you've been able to see ghosts?" I nodded. "When he attacked you, he opened up the spirit world to you. Things humans shouldn't see." I knew the attack was the cause of it, I just never knew why or how.

"Why did he attack me? And why are all these demons after me now?" He moved from the bed to the window. He leaned against the wall and gazed outside before answering me.

"You are the Vessel, Melanie." I gave him a funny look.

"A vessel?" I cracked a smile.

He turned around to look at me. Only he wasn't smiling. "You're not just a vessel. You're *the* Vessel. The only one." He sighed when I just kept looking at him liking he was crazy. "It was thought to be a rumor angels made up. Until you were born. You couldn't be touched as a child or awakened; until your eighteenth birthday."

"What?" I said stupidly. Angels? I was *the*

Vessel?

"What I'm saying is true. Your life is in danger but that much, you know. Why do you not believe what I say with everything that's happened already?" He frowned, his muscular body tensing up. The room felt smaller with him in it.

"Listen to what you are saying," I told him.

He groaned, running his hands through his messy dark hair. He looked up. "I don't understand why I have to protect you."

"You claim to be here to protect me, that's still up for debate," I added.

He looked at me like he wanted to hurt me. "You're impossible, Human. You'd be dead already if it wasn't for me."

That was true, but that didn't mean that he wasn't up to something. "Okay, explain."

"It's hard to explain to a mere human that knows nothing."

"Explain the Vessel part."

He studied the shade lamp on the nightstand.

It was getting darker in my room now that the sun was almost gone from the sky. Every second the room seemed to grow darker and my fear did with it. My lamp flickered on just as I was getting up to turn it on. I stared at him. Somehow, he turned it on.

"You're a weapon," he finally answered.

"A weapon?" I placed my arms underneath my breasts, arching one eyebrow. His eyes followed my movement and lingered on my chest a little longer than I liked. I dropped my arms back down.

"Power. No one knows anything else about it other than it being a vast amount of power. Demons love power, they crave it. Want it for themselves. Which is why they're after you and why I was sent here to protect you," he said the last part distastefully.

"This all sounds so crazy." I grabbed my head and fell back onto the bed.

"What's crazy is me having to protect you,"

he said again. I heard him move and tilted my head to see him.

He was watching me. "How did you turn on that lamp?" I asked, leaning up.

"Power," was all he offered. "I'm a busy being, I have many responsibilities. Unfortunately, that now involves looking after you so do me a favor and do as I say." He tipped his chin up. "That is, if you want to live."

I stood from the bed and walked until I was in front of him. "Who are you? If I have to see you again, I should at least know that much."

"Killian," he whispered.

"Killian." I let his name slip through my lips. As if saying his name would make everything real. "Okay, now what the heck are you Killian?"

He took a step closer to me; we were only inches apart. I leaned away, but kept my eyes locked with his. He reached for my waist to keep me from going any further. He towered his huge frame over my smaller one. I never took my eyes away from his, afraid that this was a test to see if I would look away. I wouldn't, even though I wanted to.

"Are you sure you want to know?" he whispered in my ear. I was so aware of every part of him around me that I couldn't muster up an answer. He stepped away and I could breathe again. "What do you think I am?" he asked, amused with my reddened cheeks.

"The devil," I answered immediately.

He looked repulsed. "Do not insult me like that."

I went wide-eyed. "You speak as if you know him?" That was very unsettling.

"Well..." He laughed, my lamp flickered on and off. I would be afraid if I didn't know it had to be him. He acted bored with the topic. "You can say I keep his business in check, in a way." I never noticed I was backing away from him until I fell onto my bed. "You don't have to fear me. I don't come after the living." His voice was alarming and playful all at once. "Not until you die, then I come for you."

It was hard not to feel scared. I didn't know this man. Or if he was even a man. He showed up the same day the fog had. How could I trust a stranger to protect me? My shoulders dropped in defeat.

What other choice did I have?

I looked back up. "What does that even mean?"

"I'll leave you to think about it." He smiled before disappearing before my very eyes. I blinked several times. I laughed before it turned into a cry for help. Yes, this was me giving in. My life was taking another drastic turn. Like ghosts weren't enough. Now demons? I was the Vessel? What did any of this even mean. I stared at the blurring red light of my alarm clock and rubbed the shoulder Killian healed. It wasn't like I was getting any more answers tonight.

CHAPTER FIVE

That morning I wondered if maybe I could ignore my alarm clock beeping in the distance. If I ignored the fact that I needed to get Alex up for school. If only I stopped worrying about everything and just stayed in the warmth of my bed. Maybe all my worries would go away.

Only that wasn't possible.

I couldn't stay in bed forever. I had to pee. And I would eventually get hungry. Laying down at night was never a comfort for me. It was only a reminder of how little I slept, tossing and turning every night. My own thoughts would drive me mad. Giving up wasn't an option for me, so I pulled the blanket from my face and hit snooze. I

climbed out of bed, woke Alex, and drove him to
school.

The day went in a blur, in a horrible slow-
motion kind of way. I was there but not really. My
thoughts kept me where they wanted me while my
body seemed to know everything it needed to do.
A bell rung in the distance but I was barely aware
of it.

"Melanie." Tess shook my shoulder, heaving
an irritated sound. "Melanie." She finally got my
attention. I didn't know how long she stood there
calling my name. The classroom was already
empty.

"Yeah," I mumbled. I closed the open book
on my desk, picking it up as I stood. I could hear
her flats on the concrete floor as she hurried to
catch up to me.

"Hey, are you okay?" She caught up to me as
I left the classroom, leaning in close. Her hair
caught between her lips and she pulled it away.
"You're acting weird. Well *weirder*," she pointed

out.

"I'm fine."

At our lockers, we tossed our books in before going to the cafeteria. Cheeseburgers and fries were on the menu. I ate every tasteless bite. I don't remember any of the conversations we had during that time. The rest of the school day went by just like that.

As I walked through the parking lot after school, someone caught me by the arm. I jumped, almost dropping the worn-down satchel I carried around with my books. Ryan twisted me around to face him. "Hey." I stared, feeling the mask I wore all day crumbling underneath his worried look.

Stop Melanie. You made a promise to yourself you needed to keep.

"What's wrong? Tell me, the truth." His expression deepened, his grip on my arm tightening. "Not anything but the truth."

I felt my resolve weaken. I wanted to keep him in my life, just because I was greedy for him.

But I also wanted to keep him out of my problems because he deserved normal. Now I realized how impossible that was. I was on the verge of crumbling and I wanted him to be the anchor. I needed someone to tell me everything was going to be okay.

I was scared. Afraid of myself. Of everything. So, I gave in.

"You wouldn't believe me." I teared up.

He released my arm and looked at me like I had physically hurt him. "Melanie, I understand why you're afraid to let people in. I know that better than anyone, but this is me. I've always been on your side. I believe everything you say because I know it's the truth. I don't see the things you do, but I wished I could. So, you wouldn't ever have to be alone in your world." The tears fell from my eyes, sliding down my cheeks. He placed his hands on my face and began to wipe them away. The act of kindness only made me cry harder.

"I don't have practice; you are coming home

with me and you're gonna spill your heart out. Everything." His hands were still cupping my cheeks when I nodded my reply.

———————

I pulled in Ryan's driveway, parking behind his truck. I followed him so that he wouldn't have to take me back to my car when I left. I admired their beautiful log home. It wasn't a two-story home but it was still big. I always loved log homes, something gorgeous and country about them. Ryan stepped out of his truck and smiled back at me. I smiled, it feeling real for the first time today.

Tess was out with Mike and I knew his parents weren't home. I shut my car door and followed him inside. Ryan and his dad were hunters and it was obvious when you entered the home. A bobcat mounted on one wall when you entered, resting above the fireplace. Its eyes seemed to follow me everywhere in the room, always freaking me out every time I came over.

Two deer heads were mounted on another wall. The kitchen and living room were joined in one huge room, separated by a wooden bar.

They also had a trophy room that held all their guns in two gun safes and a buffalo was mounted in that room. I wasn't a fan of hunting; I didn't have the heart to. But I did have respect for Ryan and his dad, they didn't do it just for sport. They ate what they killed.

I knew his parents were gone because their vehicles were missing but I still asked. "Where's your parents?" I slipped off my shoes by the door.

"Dad's working and Mom's probably at the grocery store or something." He tossed his keys on the wooden bar before going to his bedroom. "My rooms a mess. I wasn't expecting company." When I entered, he was picking up piles of dirty clothes scattered over the floor. I smiled as he ran to the laundry room with them. He had a few pop cans scattered in the room. He had a computer desk in one corner and a TV in front of his bed. It was very different than my clean, organized room. I didn't have a computer in my bedroom, instead I kept a large bookshelf full of books.

I laughed as he came back in the room. "It's okay, I already know you're a slob." He tossed a sock that he missed in the floor at me and I squealed, smacking it away. "Not nice," I told him, and he smiled.

Silence filled the room. We were alone in his room. I shouldn't have been so nervous. I spent many days locked away in this room with him, sometimes with Tess. But now it felt new.

I moved to the desk and sat down in the computer chair. He coughed, awkwardly and dropped down on his bed. "Let's talk." He broke the silence. I twirled around in the chair, randomly, avoiding and dreading this conversation. He stopped the chair, pulling it close to him. He looked to me for answers.

I scooped my legs up and hid my face in my knees. "I don't want you to think I'm even crazier,"

I mumbled into my knees.

He grabbed my knees so that I looked up. He looked desperate. "Have you not been listening? It's me, look how long we've been friends."

"I know," I said quickly. "I know. I'm in danger, Ryan. Things are after me." I waited, hoping and praying he didn't give me the look my parents had always given me. Like I was insane. But it never came. With every passing second all I could see was the worry I felt coming from his eyes. He believed me.

"What's after you?"

"I think demons. Or that's what he told me."

"He?" he asked, alarmed.

"Yeah, I don't know who he is-" My cell phone rang, cutting me off. I pulled it from my pocket, it was a number I didn't recognize. "Hello?" I answered.

"Do you wish for me to erase your boyfriend's memories?" Killian's harsh voice drifted through my ear.

"What?" I spoke calmly, Ryan was looking at me.

"You're about to tell him about me. And everything else that's happened. Don't. It will put him in danger." I didn't reply and stared toward Ryan. He looked to me patiently. I never imagined I'd was putting him in danger. I swallowed, stomach feeling queasy. "Not another word." The called ended. I dropped the hand that was holding the phone to my ear.

"Who was it?" he asked.

"Oh, um." I tried to think of an answer to give him. "Mom!" That also reminded me of someone I forgot. "Oh, god. Alex." I forgot to pick him up after school.

"What?" Ryan stared confused.

I hurried out of his room. He followed behind me as I stopped at the front door to slip on my shoes. "I forgot to pick Alex up after school. I was so worried about myself that I forgot about him." I sighed. "I'm a horrible sister."

Ryan stepped in front of the door. "Melanie, wait. Who were you talking about?" It took a second to remember who he was referring to. I reached for the doorknob, avoiding his eyes.

"Oh, Alex. He's been so nervous lately, always talking about demons and stuff," I lied. "It's the games he's been playing but you know me. The simplest things leave me on edge." His shoulders sagged in relief and I plastered a smile on my face.

"I was worried."

"Sorry. I got to go." He opened the door for me as I hurried to the car.

I rushed to Alex's school, driving recklessly. I parked at the door and ran inside. The principal's office was the first door on the right as I walked in.

"Can I help you?" an elderly secretary asked as she stacked papers in a pile.

"Yeah, I need to pick up Alex Rose," I told her.

She wrinkled her nose as she squinted at me.

"He's in the cafeteria. He stayed back for after-school."

"Thank you." I smiled leaving the room. I had forgot, today was one of the days of the week that he stayed back for tutoring or activities. I panicked for nothing. I walked the hallway, remembering my own childhood spent here. Brought back so many memories and the painful one I wanted to forget.

I spotted him next to a boy and cute girl as I stepped into the cafeteria. I looked at my phone and went back outside and waited. He had another thirty minutes left, I could wait. But I got sidetracked as I walked outside when I noticed a boy swinging at the playground. To anybody else it would have looked like a swing swinging by itself, surrounded by a line of others that weren't moving. Life taken so soon, made me wonder what happened to him. As if he knew I was watching him, he stopped and walked away, disappearing into nothing.

I walked to the swings, going to the first one and started swinging. I moved in a steady rhythm. Just a moment, if only this moment, I felt peace. I forgot everything else and remembered how good it felt to relax.

"You look calm for someone in so much danger," Killian's voice drifted behind me. The peace lasted all but thirty seconds. I whipped my head around as he walked around me.

"How do you always know where I am?" It was creepy. He also had known that I was at Ryan's and what I was about to tell him. I got up and started searching my body.

He frowned. "What are you doing?"

"Looking for some sort of tracker or listening device," I answered still touching every nick and curve of my body.

"I know everything you do, Melanie." His creepy factors just kept going up.

"Go away."

"I can't do that."

"Shoo!" I kicked my foot at him, feeling silly but I didn't care.

"I'm not a dog."

"Go!" I yelled.

"I can't, I'm here to keep you safe," he argued, frowning upon my behavior. I stepped back to sit down on the swing and missed it completely, falling in the dirt. He snorted.

"So much for protecting me, I could have broken something." Probably not, at this point I was picking anything to argue about.

"I doubt it," he replied. "You're going to want my help, *Human.*" There he went again.

"You know my name, stop with the *human.*" I mocked his tone when saying the word.

I saw Alex and other students walking out. I was glad and hurried away. I drove us home wishing I could forget seeing Killian. Ever.

CHAPTER SIX

Wednesday, I noticed things were changing.
The ghosts that have roamed the halls since I've
been here, were gone. Now that I thought about, I
hadn't seen Fred the day before. Or the couple. I
hadn't seen any of them since Monday. So much
was going on that I never noticed until Josh
walked by me in the hall and his ancestor wasn't
there glaring at me.

I felt uneasy. I didn't have to pick Alex up
since Mom was off today so I stayed back and
watched the boys practice on the field. It didn't
help much, the disappearance of the ghosts had me
confused. Did it have something to do with what
was happening to me?

"What happened between you and Ryan

yesterday?" Tess slurped her Dr. Pepper through a straw in the can.

I shook my head. "I acted like a total moron, how do you think it went?"

She smiled. "Really. He was on cloud nine yesterday from just having you over and to himself, even if only for a while." Don't tell me that.

I pretended to be annoyed. It only hurt. "Well, he's very sweet."

"I don't think that's what it is," she continued.

"I can't, Tess," I blurted. She stopped slurping her drink and frowned. "You know why... I could never dream of being with your brother the way I am now."

"I don't think there's anything wrong with you that needs to change."

"You're kind, Tess. Like your brother." I frowned, moving my feet across the bleachers as I stared at the field.

"I'm not kind," she mumbled.

But she was. They were nice when everyone else wasn't.

That night, I tossed and turned. I'd fall asleep only to wake right back up. Over and Over. It wasn't only this night. This was every night. I never felt rested. I stared at the ceiling, thinking of Tess and Ryan, how much they cared. How much I wanted to let them in but couldn't. I was a danger to them and I was in danger myself but I had no one. Not even they could help ease my mind now.

Could I believe what Killian told me? I asked myself every second of the day and always got the same answer. Yeah. I've always seen ghosts, now one was trying to kill me. Something else tried as well. I guess that's why it was so easy for me to believe a complete stranger.

But how could I trust him to protect me? What was he and why did he have to protect me when he clearly didn't want to?

I squeezed my eyes shut trying to turn off my brain. I wanted my mind to quieten.

"You look as if you are straining, not sleeping." His voice always had a darkness about it. I opened my eyes and found him standing next to the window. My mind always went back to how could he get in here, which was silly since I was positive he wasn't normal. And he used power.

I rose, feeling angry. "Get out," I ordered, but my voice never made a sound. I grabbed my throat. "What's wrong with my voice?" I mouthed because the words never came out. I panicked then glared at Killian. "What did you do?"

He smirked. "I knew you'd scream. Can't have your mom hearing a man's voice in your room, now can I?"

My heart beat wildly, not from fear but anger. How did he take my voice? A small part wanted to believe that he was here to protect me, like he said. But his actions always left me confused. The desperate part of me needed to believe that he would protect me. The one that didn't care he was a stranger. Just wanted someone to help me. "My voice, give it back!" I mouthed.

"I think I like you this way." He walked to my bookshelf, his eyes skimming over my collection. He pulled out one of my favorite erotic novels. "So, you're this kind of girl?" He sounded surprised and I blushed. Even my mom didn't know what books I read, she just knew I read. Not even Tess or Ryan. I kept that part a secret, afraid of what others would think of me. "Then again, I can see it. The things you try to hide." I was glad the room was mostly dark, the lamp cast a small glow across the room. I hoped it wasn't enough to show him my blushed skin.

"What are you doing here?" He turned back to the bookshelf as I asked. The words never came from my lips, the room stayed deathly quiet except the rustling of books.

Somehow, he knew what I had mouthed despite having his back facing me. "It's boring when you don't know that I'm with you. Following you." He left the bookshelf. His eyes trapped mine as he strode toward the bed. For some reason, it caused my heart to beat in entirely different way. I pulled the quilt up to my chin when he sat down beside me. "Why look at me like that?" He arched a dark eyebrow. I still didn't know him and this was the second time he broke into my room. How else was I supposed to look at him? He studied my hands gripping the quilt before looking away. "You don't have to be afraid. Not of me." He stood quickly, moving away from the bed, suddenly caring that he may have crossed the line too far.

I watched, curious of him. His actions had changed, odd and out of place, like he was racking his brain on what he planned to do next. "Is it weird for me to be in your room?" I looked shocked. Did he really just ask that question?

"It's creepy. I don't know you." I was surprised that my voice was back. "Even if I did, you're breaking and entering."

"I don't get the humans view on privacy," he told me, fumbling with his words. "Things are different back home but I do enjoy my own privacy every now and then." He raked his hand through his hair, looking different than all the times before. "I don't mean to make you fear me. I only want you to understand. And I guess I was a bit bored with watching you, so I hadn't noticed how late it was or that it would upset you for me to enter your room. You are female."

"Are you really always watching me?" I asked nervously.

"Not physically but in a sense. I follow your movements so I know when there's danger."

"You also heard my conversation with Ryan, you stopped me from telling him."

"I listen when I need to."

"That's invasion of privacy," I pointed out.

"I have no choice. I could keep you close and you wouldn't have to wonder when I was watching and listening..."

"No, thanks," I replied immediately. I got the feeling he was joking, but it was also him telling the truth. He watched me. "But, really." I looked up to him, meeting his eyes. "What are you, I get that you're not human. You're always pointing out that I am one," I paused. "Are you... a demon?" I whispered.

"I am," he said then quickly added, "but I haven't been one in a very long time." Now I was confused. What was he then? "I will let you sleep. I didn't mean to invade your privacy, for that, I apologize. I simply noticed you weren't sleeping..." He drifted off like he wasn't sure why he was explaining himself.

"I don't sleep." He cocked his head in disbelief. "I mean, I can't. Hardly ever. Since the attack and being able to see ghosts, I can't sleep more than a few minutes at a time." I didn't know why I said it. It wasn't for him to pity me, I hated pity. I just thought... he'd understand.

"That explains why you always look so frail." He stepped next to the bed and placed his knee next to me. He hesitated above me causing me to feel anxious.

"What are you doing?" I looked up.

"Do you wish to sleep? A good night's worth?" he asked.

I slowly nodded. "Why, what are you going to do?" I knew he was about to do something.

"I'm going to help you sleep, lie down and get comfortable." He leaned over me. I did as he told me. I laid my head on the pillow, getting as comfortable as I could with him hovering over me. "Will you stop looking as if I'm going to attack you. We've moved past that already, I'm not interested."

"I got it!" I spoke harshly, looking away. I could see his grin from the corner of my eye. "What if the demons attack me while I'm asleep," I whispered nervously.

"That's what I'm here for." Those five words and all my worries disappeared. "Close your eyes." I listened and closed them. I felt the warmth of his palm touch my forehead then I fell asleep.

CHAPTER SEVEN

For the first time, I overslept. My bed felt so good. I snuggled the pillow, squishing my face in its warmth. Some noise blared in a faraway distance. Too far away for my conscious to care until Mom opened the door and yelled. I jumped, twisting in the quilt, tangling myself in it. I fell onto the floor with a loud thump.

I hit the snooze button on my alarm as Mom stood at the door. "You never oversleep." She was surprised. So was I.

I was going to be late for my first class. There was no way I was getting to school on time. I rushed anyway, running around like a chicken with its head cut off. I brushed my teeth as I placed my hair in a messy bun. Not that my hairstyle was any different, I always wore it up. I put on a pink blouse and leggings, not what I usually wore, but all my usual clothes were in the hamper waiting to be washed. Mom was rushing Alex.

"Sorry, I must have been sleeping good." Better than good. I even felt energized. Whatever Killian did last night had me sleeping like a baby. I hurried downstairs trying to remember where I left my car keys.

"I'm glad to see you sleeping so good, I always worry you don't get enough." Mom chirped. I picked up the junk mail to look underneath them.

"Have you seen my keys?" I asked.

"Beside the microwave." She pointed with her head toward the kitchen. "Go ahead and get to school. I'll take your brother."

After finding my keys, I went back to the hallway to put on my flips-flops. They weren't many days left that I'd get to wear them; the morning and nights were already chilly. "Are you sure?" I grabbed the doorknob.

She smiled. "Yeah. You do enough as it is. Go."

I only missed first period and the rest of the day went by quickly. Maybe that had something to do with the way I felt. I was in a better mood than I normally was. Sleep was amazing. But the fact that none of the ghosts were at school had me wary.

At lunch, I grabbed every food offered and joined my usual group at the table. I found myself laughing at the jokes Mike told us, when normally I didn't. I smiled and held conversations.

"You look good today." Ryan took notice and smiled.

"Yeah. I slept good last night," I replied.

"Are you sure that's the reason?" I gave him a funny look, trying to think of what other reason I would be in such a good mood. No, sleep was my new lover. "You just seem so happy."

"You know I barely sleep, last night I slept all night and even overslept. I feel refreshed is all." I grinned at him.

"You're right, it's just surprising but a good surprise. The kind that's nice to see." He scooted his chair closer. His obvious intentions always left me uncomfortable when I was trying so hard to keep a distance from him.

"Melanie," Tess interrupted and I gladly turned to look at her. Her brother was making one of his moves that left me with butterflies.

"Yeah," I replied quickly.

"The party's Saturday so there's no backing out. A lot of people have already been invited," she warned me.

"I'm not." I sighed.

"Good." She smiled before giving Mike a kiss.

I kept my focus on them instead of the boy next to me trying for my attention. His intentions were very clear.

"Melanie," Ryan spoke into my ear. I wanted to ignore him, but that would be giving myself away.

I turned my head slowly. He was closer than I realized. "Yeah?" I mumbled.

"The party Saturday." He stared at my lips when he spoke.

"Yeah?"

"We should…," his voice faded again.

"Yeah?" I said again, because apparently, that was the only word I knew.

Something made a loud thump in the cafeteria causing everyone to jump. I looked away from Ryan to find what caused the noise. A tray fell on the floor a table across from us. The girl looked down at the tray confused, as if she had no clue what happened. The chatter started back as everyone lost interest in what happened. A cafeteria lady walked out to clean up the mess and something caught my eyes as I was turning back to the table.

"Did she do it on purpose?" Tess wondered.

I scanned the room for what I saw and shook

my head. I could have sworn I saw Killian leaving the cafeteria. I was probably wrong. "Who are you looking for?" Ryan asked.

"No one." I shrugged my shoulders and turned back to the table.

———————

I was brushing my blonde hair that night wishing everyday could be as normal as today felt. No ghosts, meant no worries. Ryan felt closer, but I wasn't sure if that was a good thing. Killian said it was dangerous. I sighed.

But the dread was back as I laid my head down on the pillow. Tonight wouldn't be like last night. I was already afraid of where my mind might wander. If Killian were here...

No! What was I thinking?

I couldn't ask him to do that again. I didn't even know exactly what he done. It could be dangerous. He was dangerous. He wasn't even human, he already admitted that he was once a demon. I didn't know what that made him now.

But it wasn't like I could get in touch with him even if I wanted to... I tossed in my bed. This wasn't working. I sighed and rose from back up. Was he going to visit again? I glanced around my room. Wait, did I want him to come?

The night was long, I tossed and turned. Killian never came. And morning arrived and the day was the same as the day before. No ghosts, I felt normal but not as lively. Then it was another repeat of last night trying to fall asleep.

Friday evening after school, a thought hit me. Maybe I couldn't see ghosts anymore. Building up my nerves, I decided to go to a cemetery to check. I felt jittery and almost lost my nerves a few times on the way there. I stayed clear of places that ghosts might be, but I was even more stressed that I couldn't see them so I had to know. Did the ghosts leave school or could I not see them anymore? I hadn't been anywhere besides school and home to know. I parked beside the road and walked to the cemetery, opening a small wooden gate to enter. I chose this cemetery because it was small, about ten graves. Less ghosts.

I shivered even though it was still warm outside. I walked quietly through the wooden fence. I didn't need to go further. I could see the graves perfectly. This was close enough. The place hadn't been taken care of in a while, the fence was falling over and the grass was overgrown. It'd be dangerous to even try to walk any further into the high grass, there could be snakes. The pine trees around the cemetery blocked any sunlight from coming through, making it dark and creepy.

I waited but nothing popped up yet. Before I lost my nerve, I called out, "Hello?" If anybody had been around, I would have looked like an idiot. But this place was a good distance away from any homes. It was just an old graveyard beside the road.

My skin felt damp from the heat and possibly my agitation, every second that passed I was beginning to think I couldn't see them anymore. I should leave. As I turned, I heard something. Like something was being dragged. I turned my head slowly to look back.

A young soldier moved through the grass, limping as he did. It wasn't until he was out of the tall grass that I saw the way his leg was twisted and mangled, deforming it. He dragged it behind him as he walked. Half his face was gone from what might have been a gunshot wound and his right hand was missing. I ran away, but only came upon another ghost. It was woman crying nonstop, cradling her arms like she was holding a baby, but nothing was there. She stopped when she noticed me before her crying got worse. "Please, my baby. My baby," she screamed at me. I backed away from her and went through the soldier.

It was scary that I could never touch them but they could me. The soldier grabbed my arm with his only hand left and stared down at it. "Give me this arm," he moaned, staring down at my arm like he was about to tear it off. I screamed and jerked away from him. I ran through the gate and locked myself in my car and drove away.

There was no way I was sleeping tonight. I could still feel the cold touch of the soldier and shivered. I tried to talk to Alex, it worked for a good hour, but he went to sleep and I was left alone and awake. I was an idiot for thinking things had changed. Mom was at work, not that I could talk to her about anything.

It was two in the morning; I had given up sleep around midnight and grabbed a book to read. Being tired but not being able to sleep, I guess that meant I had insomnia? As tired as I felt, the moment I rested my eyes I saw everything I feared.

I closed the book. "Killian." I didn't know why I whispered it. I wasn't expecting him to be listening.

"Melanie." I jumped despite being the one that called him here. He stood at the end of my bed.

"You scared me," I mumbled, still a bit

spooked. He shrugged his shoulders.

"What do you want?" he asked. I rose from my belly and straightened my back. It popped a few times from being in that position for so long.

"What makes you think I want something?" Of course, I did. Why else would I call his name?

"You mean, you called me in your room this late for nothing at all." He tested me, smirking.

I went all defensive. "You are supposed to protect me, right?" I challenged, moving off the bed and closer to him. Once I was close, I pushed my index finger into his chest. "I was attacked today, where were you?" His grin turned to pure mischief. I was surprised at how young it made him look. And playful.

"You mean your encounter with the ghosts at the cemetery?" His booming laughter filled the room, fueling my anger. How could he laugh when I had been so afraid? He stopped when he saw the murderous glare I was giving him. "Relax, you weren't in danger. They couldn't harm you."

"One of them touched me," I argued.

"Melanie, what did you really feel? Think about it, it was the chill of your body going through his. He reached for you, but could never actually hold you there." I tried to think back to what happened, was I wrong? I was so sure he grabbed my arm. "You felt the pull of him trying, for him to hurt a human, he would need to become a poltergeist. He wasn't at that stage and he never will be." I sighed. "But thanks for the entertainment, it was quite interesting watching you freak out when they went for you." I opened my mouth to snap at him. "Answer me this, if you're so afraid of ghosts. Why did you go to that cemetery?" he questioned.

I closed it back, pulling at a strand of my hair that trailed over my breasts. "I haven't seen any of the ghosts at school lately, I thought maybe... I couldn't see them anymore." Big mistake. It sounded stupid now that I thought about it.

"It's because of me." He moved away from me and I followed him with my eyes.

"What do you mean?"

"Ghosts run from me."

"Why?" He flopped down on my bed and ruffled his hands through his hair.

"Ghosts don't cross me if they wish to stay in the human world." He started rummaging through my nightstand. Another invasion of privacy, I rolled my eyes. But I was also becoming a tad curious of him as well. I wasn't afraid of him as much as I should be. He oozed danger like it was a part of him. But there was something that felt human. I shook my head, erasing all thoughts of him. What was I thinking?

"You're not going to tell me what you are?" I asked again.

He pulled out a notebook from the stand and I reached out to grab it from him. "You will know soon enough." Another blank answer. I bent over to grab the notebook as he raised it in the air. My foot slipped on the carpet when I rose too quickly to take it. His arms went out for me so that my head wouldn't hit the stand. Air rushed out of my lungs as he jerked me back. I fell onto him. My head hit his chin and he grunted. I moved my head rubbing it as I met his eyes.

"Sorry." My words got lost somewhere in the depths of his eyes. Our noses met, I realized I was practically in his lap but I didn't move. Not yet. Something about the way he looked at me stole my reason to. He wasn't human, but he was a male and I was being reminded of that as I felt the hard press of him underneath my hands as I held us apart by pressing against his chest. He was scary. He was...

He looked different up close, I couldn't look away.

Something stirred in my chest and that's when I chose to lean away. The room was quiet as Killian watched me move away. I turned my head, faking a yawn, trying to ease the weird tension in the room. Everything felt strange. "Is your head okay?" he asked.

I remembered the reason for the fall and snatched the book from his hand. "All that for a notebook?" he teased, but something about the way he spoke seemed softer. Or maybe it was just me.

"I scribble nonsense when I can't sleep. Nothing I want people to read." Which was something I did a lot. Words were my comfort; with a good book, I could escape all my troubles. Somewhere along the way, I started jotting down things of my own.

"I see." The lamp started flickering.

"Will you stop doing that?" I asked nervously.

"The dark isn't so bad, Melanie." He knew I was afraid of the dark. "I should go." I frowned as soon as he said that. "You're disappointed." He noticed, a hint of softness touching his lips. Maybe even satisfaction. "Why?"

"Just..." I trailed off.

"Sleep, humans need it." He patted for me to lay down. He still sat on the bed. I gave him a hopeful nod and moved onto the bed beside him. I laid down turning my body in the direction he sat. "Are you comfortable?" he asked. I grabbed my favorite quilt and placed it over me before nodding. He twisted his body to face me better. The last thing I remembered was his palm touching my forehead.

CHAPTER EIGHT

My cell phone woke me up around noon. I lifted my head up. My hair covered a good portion of my face as I felt for it on the stand. "Hello?" I answered groggily.

"Are you still asleep?" Tess asked, surprised. "When are you coming over? Just tell your mom that you're spending the night," she added.

"I know," I grumbled. She was always lecturing me like a child, like I didn't know how to lie to my mom? I did it every day while pretending to be normal. But this was different and I never told a fib just to go to a party. I could probably tell her the truth and she'd be happy that I was doing normal teenage things.

"Okay, don't take all day." She hung up.

I showered and ate a bite before leaving, arriving about two hours later. I told Mom I was staying at Tess's, which wasn't a lie. I just excluded the part about us going to a party. When I walked in, Tess was wearing a pair of shorts that barely covered her butt cheeks. It was going to be chilly tonight, I hoped that wasn't what she was wearing to the party. I wore a white tank top and jeans and brought a thin jacket to put on when it got chilly.

While waiting to go to the party, we sat in her room listening to music. She painted my fingernails and toes. After a long argument about makeup, I finally gave in and let her apply a little on me. She always looked pretty, so maybe she could do some magic on me.

"I'm leaving Tessa." Her mom peeked her head in the door. "You girls be good and I'll be back sometime tomorrow night."

"We will," Tess replied.

"Tell your brother for me," she said, shutting the door behind her.

Speaking of Ryan, I glanced around her room. They were both unorganized and messy. She had a television in her room and a pink laptop sitting on a desk, hidden under a pile of clothes. Her iPad was next to her feet on the bed. I knew their parents were well off when it came to money but rarely where they home. "Where is your brother?" I asked.

"He went with Mike and his brother to get the alcohol." I arched my eyebrow and she added. "Mike's brother is twenty-four." My mouth went up in a O. So, that's how they were getting it. I felt a little nervous about tonight. I felt like I was about to do something bad just because I wanted to drink alcohol at least once before something succeeded in killing me.

"Will there be a lot of people?" I asked.

"Probably a few from school and Mike's brother." She shrugged, sliding off her bed and running to her closet. She rummaged through her clothes. "Found them!" she squealed. By 'them' she meant a pair of ripped jeans.

There were more than a few people. Ryan drove us, the drive took twenty minutes. It wasn't that the drive was a long one, but the bumpy dirt road going up several steep hills made it take longer. The strip job was no longer a mining place, grass covered the open field. It was surrounded by small mountains that held four-wheeler tracks going up and down. Everything was still the color of summer, but up here in the mountains, some of the trees were already beginning to change to fall.

Once we arrived, I stepped out of Ryan's huge truck. There was a lot of people I recognized from school and there was even more that I didn't. I wasn't a social butterfly like Tess or Ryan so I didn't know these people, even the ones I went to school with. I moved around the truck awkwardly. I was glad I chose walking shoes. The grass was spotted, missing some in spots while in other places it was high. I watched Tess skip through the grass in flip-flops.

"I told you to wear tennis shoes," I said as I walked behind her.

"You know I don't wear any type of shoe unless it's flip-flops, boots, or flats," she replied.

I shook my head. Ryan met me at the tailgate of his truck with a goofy grin on his face. I smiled back. The sky was darkening and people moved their trucks into a circle, providing light while someone started a fire. Music blared, pouring out of the back of a truck. That was also where all the alcohol was. It was a lot, my definition of a lot and someone else could be different but I couldn't imagine everyone drinking that much.

But...

There were quite a few people here, some drinking and others already drunk. "Well," I said. People bumped and rubbed against each other as they danced. The grass flattened where they danced, the steady movement of everyone's shoes making their own dance floor. Not only were there grinding as people danced, tongues collided, and other body parts meshed together as well. Girls humped each other's legs, well they were dancing, but it looked entirely like humping. A few guys stood to the side, watching the girls and laughing at someone's joke.

"What do you think? Too much?" Ryan asked in my ear. I met his eyes and smiled. I honestly didn't know what to think. I was out of my element.

Tess pressed into me and grabbed my arm. "Let's go grab you a drink." She smiled and led us to the tailgate of the truck that held all the alcohol. Ryan followed behind us. Tess picked up a bottle and cup, filling it up before handing it to me. "Here, drink up." She grinned.

I brought it to my nose and sniffed. Woo, it was strong. Smelt nasty. "What is it?" I hesitated.

"Vodka."

They watched as I brought the cup to my

mouth and took a drink. I sputtered, but swallowed it down. It burned my neck and stomach as it slid down. "That was horrible."

Ryan grabbed my cup. "Here, orange juice or Cola will make it better."

"Hello gorgeous." Mike sneaked up behind Tess wrapping his arms around her. She leaned back and smiled.

"Orange juice or coke?" Ryan asked. I sighed, did I have to choose either? This was what I came to do.

"Surprise me," I told him. He picked the orange juice. After pouring some into my cup, he handed it back to me. I took another sip. Much better. Not something I was in love with, though. I took another drink.

"Better?" he asked, grabbing a beer and taking a huge gulp.

"A little."

"Come on, Melanie. Let's dance." For someone that wanted me with her brother, she loved taking me away from him. I laughed when I caught the desperate look on his face as she pulled me away.

Then he caught me by surprise. "Not so fast." He grabbed my arm and it caused me to spill some of my drink.

Tess grumbled before she let me go. "Let's go, Mike." She latched onto his arm and disappeared into the crowd of music and laughter. Someone bumped my back pushing me to Ryan. He caught my arms using the opportunity to pull me closer. I squeezed the drink between us and took another drink.

"Do you want to dance?" I looked at everyone rubbing against each other and twirling. Some were acting ridiculous.

"Um." I hesitated.

"Come on." He pulled us closer to the others. He moved me to the rhythm of the music. I didn't know what I was doing, so I just followed after him. After picking up a few hip movements and random body jerking, I was starting to realize why so many people danced freakishly. I was smiling and took another drink. I felt free.

Ryan pulled me closer, I let him. I went for another drink but there were none. "I need more." I held my cup out to him. He grinned before he went to get it for me. He came back with more and we danced some more. My second cup was empty before I knew it. So, he got me another and I drunk it.

The giggles started. Everything was suddenly hilarious.

Wow, I tossed my head back and laughed. I didn't even care that some dude kept bumping into my back. Someone touched my butt. No... I was positive I was being groped. I wrapped my arms around Ryan's neck and laughed. "Did you touch my butt?" Ah, there again. Someone touched it again! I grabbed his hands and studied them intensely.

Again! I held his hands and looked

confused. "Huh?" Who was touching my butt then? I looked back, but we drifted a foot away from the others.

He laughed. "Come here."

"My butt," I said. He pulled me away.

"You keep leaning against Brian's truck, no one's touching your butt. You're drunk and can hardly stand," he told me. I looked back again. Sure enough, there was a truck.

I grinned at it. "You ole' truck, you." I was talking to the truck, trying to walk to it but staggered. I tried to stay still but funny thing, the ground kept moving. Or was it me? I just knew I was going to fall so I held my hands out as if I were swimming, moving them around vigorously in front of me until I snorted.

Woo.

I leaned backwards. Ryan grabbed my arm. "Okay, I think you need to sit for a while."

I was still fighting the air, keeping myself afloat when I said. "Am not." Then twirl-tripped into him trying to get up in his face.

I caught his smile as he led me somewhere and sat my butt on something. I looked down. I was sure this was the truck that was getting all touchy with me earlier. I grinned. "Stay here for a second." I was going to ask where he was going, but my words weren't coming out. I fell backwards in the truck bed and thought I was never going to pull my drunken-self back up. My head swam when I tried to make sense of what I was looking at. People dancing? That was some twisty moves I'd never seen before. Or nope, just everything's spinning because of the alcohol.

Someone moved to me. I squinted hard, trying to make the person out. It was a woman. Pretty redhead. She was staring at everyone until I burped. It caught her attention. That was when I noticed the other half of her face was missing. How crazy looking, I laughed. I pointed at her face. Her clothes were old and worn down. She must be a ghost. "You only have half your face," I slurred, her eyes widened.

"You see me."

"Unfortunately," I nodded, kicking my feet back and forth on the tailgate.

"You see me." She moved closer to me.

"I see you're not very bright, missing half your brain and all." I pointed at her head before grabbing my stomach. "That's what I said, didn't I?" I felt sick.

"I shall possess your body." Alarms went off in my drunken mind, but it took several more seconds after that before I realized I was in danger. I jumped off the truck only to crumble to my knees. It took a lot of work to figure out how my limbs worked. I looked above me as the redhead moved closer. She disappeared and I dropped my head. Boots appeared in my view and I looked back up to see a very angry looking Killian. I tried to smile, but it felt awkward—all goofy and wrong. I laughed.

I was safe now.

He grabbed my arms and forced me to stand on my feet. "You're a mess." He glared. I gave him a snooty look back. I heard him mutter something about someone being a pain under his breath.

Then an awful urge hit, I bent my legs inward and squirmed. "I have to pee," I told him.

"Why are you telling me?" he asked warily. Oh, I was going to burst if I didn't do something. I grabbed the button on my jeans. He grabbed my wrist. "What are you doing?"

I looked at him as if he were stupid. "I told you, I have to PEE!"

Killian grumbled a few bad words while running his hand through that wild hair of his. Okay, I liked his hair. Pressure hit causing pain in my stomach. "There are people all around you. You want everyone to see you while you take a piss," he asked, and I couldn't figure out what the big deal was. He sighed. "Never mind, you're drunk. I'd doubt you'd care but you would in the morning." He scooped me up in his arms.

"What are you doing?" I asked.

"Finding you a place to piss." I smiled. He was so sweet.

"Thank you. My bladder and I really thank you." I moved into his face to make sure he knew just how thankful I was. He smiled and looked up to the sky.

"What the bloody hell am I doing here?" he muttered toward the sky.

"Helping me pee," I answered. "Obviously." Even I knew the answer to that.

He took us far from the party so that I could pee. It was dark, I couldn't see my own hand in front of me. He stood me on my feet and held my shoulders in case I was to fall. "I can't see."

"Which is a good thing. If you were sober, you wouldn't want people to see you." I huffed at him before I unbuttoned my pants. I pulled my jeans down and squatted. I felt instant relief as the pressure in my stomach disappeared. I finished, but realized what I had done. "Uh-oh."

"What?" He sighed.

"I think I peed on my shoes." He let out a pleasant laugh behind me. I almost fell trying to stand back up, but he caught me under my arms from the back. I grinned in the darkness. A guy was standing behind me and my pants were to my knees. There was no way he could see anything it was so dark, but my mind was in the gutter. "Are you stepping in my pee?"

"No."

I bent down to pull up my jeans and staggered back against Killian. My naked rump rubbed against him. I felt the cool touch of his jeans against my flesh. I quickly pulled them up before turning around to where he was. The action sobered me up some but not enough to shut my mouth up. "My butt rubbed against you." When he didn't reply, I asked, "Did you see anything?"

"Melanie." The alarm in his voice caused me to stiffen. "It's time to leave. Now." He shoved me forward, back toward the party.

"What? Why?" I leaned my head back to look at him as he pushed us forward. I tripped over my foot and with his hands already against my back, he caught me from falling.

"You're in danger. Here, time to sober you up." He twirled me around and touched his thumb to my forehead. My mind cleared, the dizziness left. His piercing glare scared me, that's how I knew I'd sobered. "Let's go." He started pushing me forward again and took us back to the party raging on. "Find the ones you came with and tell them to take you home."

"Is it more demons?" I asked, afraid.

He nodded. "Yeah. Fear has sent them after you."

"Fear?" I asked.

"Melanie, there you are." I caught sight of Ryan squeezing through people to get to me. His smile dropped when he noticed Killian holding onto my arm. "Who are you?" He eyed Killian head to toe and there was a lot to look at. Killian wasn't bothered by it.

"Take her home," he ordered Ryan. I sighed, palming my forehead. He was going to make Ryan angry.

"What the hell?" He got up into Killian's face, full of anger despite him being a lot bigger and taller than he was. Ryan wasn't someone to back down but I knew this wasn't entirely Ryan. It was the alcohol. "Who the fuck are you?" Then turned to me. "How do you know this piece of—"

"I'd watch what comes out of your mouth next," Killian's voice boomed with anger.

"It's hard to explain," I jumped in. His expression went from anger, to shock, then to that of hurt as he looked at me. I felt a pang of guilt hit my stomach. Ryan was analyzing the situation in his head, I watched as his eyes made assumptions of me and Killian.

"There's no time." Killian pulled me, directing me through the crowd.

"Tell everyone to leave." I looked back to

tell Ryan who looked as if he was about to blow.

"Which one is his truck?" Killian asked.

"What the hell?" Ryan roared behind us. Killian stopped and turned around, his expression never changed, but I knew he was growing impatient. I could feel his grip tightening on my arm and the vein in his neck jumped.

"The truck," Killian said calmly.

"Like hell I'm telling you," Ryan spat.

Killian's body seemed to momentarily fade, changing into something else—BUT it happened so quickly I thought I might have saw wrong. His patience was gone with Ryan. Ryan had an odd look on his face as he stared at Killian. Did he see the change in his appearance as well?

Killian grabbed his head. Was he in pain? "Melanie, she's in danger." He forced the words out. "You need to get her somewhere safe."

"Wait, what about everyone else?" I asked.

"When you leave, they will be safe." He lifted his head from his hand. I somehow knew he was telling me the truth.

"What...," Ryan started.

"Ryan, please," I pleaded. "If he says I'm in danger, I am." I stared at him until he finally sighed.

"Just what is going on?" He was hurt and confused, but I didn't have time to explain to him.

"Later," I promised.

"Let me find Tess." Ryan disappeared to find her.

I led Killian to Ryan's truck. He opened the door, scooped me up, and tossed me inside the passenger seat. Ryan was back dragging a very drunk Tess. She fought him as he opened the backdoor and slung her into the backseat. "Take me back to my boyfriend," she whined.

"I think not," he replied, fighting off her legs as she kicked him.

Killian strode around the front of the truck and climbed into the driver's side. "He doesn't actually think I'm going to let him drive my truck?" Ryan asked in disbelief.

"Get in." Killian told him. "Keys?"

"Listen—"

"Ryan." I moved my body around in the seat to look at him. He took one look at me and sighed. He reached for his pocket and tossed the keys to Killian. Killian started the truck as Ryan climbed in the back with Tess and slammed the door.

"Now, what's really going on?" Ryan moved a giggling Tess to where he could press himself in between the front seats. I looked to Killian. Did he plan to tell them? "You know Melanie sees ghosts." Killian stated and Ryan nodded.

"Yep!" Tess burped in the back. "Our Mel-Mel here can see ghosts. She's gonna grow up and be a ghostbuster." She had the hiccups. I cringed at the old nickname she used to call me when we were younger. He ignored her remark, driving reckless through the mountains. We hit every bump and hole on the ground as we drove off-road. Ryan's head hit the top once and I held on for dear life. All I could see of Tess in the back was her hair bouncing around.

"Why are you driving like a madman, I've yet to see any danger?" I gripped the seat tighter as I glared at him.

"I'm going to throw up." Tess sounded sick.

Ryan groaned and Killian slammed on the brake and slid us sideways. My head bounced off the window. He started back the other way. "They're here," he told us and my stomach bottomed out.

"Who?" Ryan asked. Maybe it was because of the adrenaline pumping through my veins, but I wasn't as afraid as I thought I should be. His driving was scaring me a little, though. A gurgling sound came from the back. Tess threw up all over the back seat and into the floor. It stunk like alcohol and stomach acid. I fanned my face. I looked back to see her staring intensely through the back window. "What is that?"

I looked to where she was pointing. Five

furry and very large creatures waited for us. "Wolf demons," Killian answered. They were disgusting looking and hairless on the chest and face. They were filthy and dirty looking. Their snout was long and pointed downward, revealing ugly yellow teeth visible even from this distance. They were as tall as Killian. No bigger. The worst part was the bend of their knees, instead of bending frontward like humans, they bent backwards. One jumped, disappearing somewhere.

"Werewolves?" I scrunched my nose up trying to figure them out.

"No, these are from the Underworld. They are vicious demons. That is their true and only form." I looked back nervously as they all jumped into the sky, splitting up. A thump sounded on top of the truck causing me to jump. I looked up. One was on top of the truck.

"What the hell!" Ryan muttered. "Are they really demons?"

Killian twitched in the driver's seat like he

did at the party. He didn't look good; I wasn't sure if I should be more worried about him or the demons. "Are you okay?" I asked. Claws slammed into my window, busting it. I moved away from the window as the razor-sharp claws came at me. The furry hand caught my shoulder and tried to pull me out the window. I let out a cry as I felt Ryan pull me back. Then I watched Killian's hand in horror and fascination as he leaned over to grab the demons hand and crushed it. The wolf demon yelped, falling off the truck. But what held my attention was Killian's hand. I met his eyes anxiously.

His skin looked sweaty. He was pale and bright like his skin was close to bursting. It was like he was having some inner battle that couldn't be seen. "Killian..." My voice gave away my fear and I knew Ryan was staring at his hand too. "Your hand." I pointed, moving my hand away and scooting away from him. Only his hand wasn't normal. His skin was gone, no muscle or tendons—nothing but a white skeletal hand and fingers. A blue light hovered around his fingers, circling around it like it was a part of him.

"This is why I didn't want you to know... but I knew you'd eventually have to. Still, I didn't want to... show you." He clenched his teeth, barely able to drive or speak. "Didn't... Want... To... Scare...You." A demon jumped on the truck's hood and two more jumped each side. I slid into Killian's side as one of their clawed hands came through the window after me.

He slammed on the brake. The two on the side fell off, but the one on the hood held on. "What's happening to you?" I asked despite the danger lurking outside.

"Ryan, take the wheel," he growled before tossing his head back. His flesh faded in and out, rippling into a skeletal being. He caught hold of his changing and looked forward. "Stay in the truck, I'll take care of the demons." He looked to make sure I was listening. I nodded, weakly. "I can't fight it, he wants out."

He threw the door open, stepped toward the demon on the hood and grabbed him by the tail. He flipped around trying to attack him, but Killian got a grip on his neck and tossed him as if he were nothing but air. One reached into the busted window and pulled me by the hair. I screamed and Ryan moved over me, taking the demon by the arm, but it was already pulling me out the window. My back caught on the broken shards of glass and I cried out. "Melanie!" Ryan screamed. The pressure from the demon pulling my hair was gone but I fell from the window. I got on my feet as a laugh echoed beside me, familiar yet so different. I turned to see a skeletal figure digging his boned fingers into the demon's chest. He wore a black cloak over his body. When the demon's body went limp, he removed his hand from its chest, dropping it to the ground. He faced me. No eyes, a blue glow moved around his body underneath his cloak.

I was afraid. I stepped back until my back

hit the truck. I knew who he was but right now, I couldn't believe it. I was terrified. Even more than I was of the three wolf demons hovering behind him. How could something with no eyes make it feel as if it was seeing straight through me. Like I was being stripped bare and he was peering into my soul. His boned hand grabbed me, cold to the touch.

His eyeless expression peered into mine before jerking open the door and shoving me back inside. I twisted myself around in the seat. "Stay." His voice boomed with power. The same as Killian's but echoing with darkness. He slammed the door shut and strode to the front of the truck.

Three wolf demons danced around him, keeping a safe distance, deciding the right moment to attack. They looked between one another, one backing away unsure and afraid but the biggest protested with a howl. They weren't going to stop. Ryan sat in the driver's side watching with both disbelief and amazement. "Melanie, what is he?"

Ryan asked.

I shook my head. "I don't know," I whispered, yet something about the way he looked was familiar. Like I'd seen it before.

Bones held out his hand and a silver object took form, shaping and stretching, becoming a weapon. It was a long, dark-silver rod that grew longer than the length of him. A long, pointed, silver tip—not a sword I've ever seen before—formed a bladed weapon, curving down. The blade was massive. I didn't know anything about swords, but it wasn't like anything I'd seen before. More ancient.

"A scythe," Ryan gasped, fascinated.

One of the demons attacked, Bones brought the scythe up and the entire weapon changed. It morphed into a dark, thick chain that caught the demon in midair and slung him to the ground at his feet. It morphed again, a normal sword. Bones brought the blade down over the demon's throat. There was a nasty gurgling sound, blood coughed from its mouth and spilled from the neck wound. Bones twisted the blade in its neck, the demon never moved again. The last two demons learned from the first mistake and jumped, disappearing into the darkness.

Something began to travel out of the dead demon's body. The black mass poured up from its body, circling the blade. It began flowing into the sword until nothing was left. "Your soul shall never rest. Never find comfort or peace. You are but a mere part of my blade, a weapon," Bones spoke down at his weapon.

He turned his hooded head toward the truck. "Ryan," I whispered quickly, grabbing his arm and smacking him. He caught on and reached for the manual-stick shift. He started toward us, large steps as if he knew. "Get us the hell out of here." I didn't have to speak twice, he spun the truck around and sped off.

I kept my head turned as Ryan drove to see if he was following us, but it was too dark to see anything. Tess was passed out in the backseat and I couldn't believe she slept through all that. I knew I was running from Killian, but that didn't change how scary he was. That was something else entirely. My skin chilled just thinking of him.

"You need to tell me what's going on?" Ryan drove us down the mountain. Away from Bones/Killian, away from the demons, and the party that I hoped was safe. I rubbed my forehead, I could feel the headache starting.

"What else can I tell you?" I opened my hand and sighed. "You've seen enough, Ryan. Demons are after me!"

"Jesus, Melanie, you could have been hurt if not for," he cut off. "How long has this been happening?"

"The night before my birthday. Killian said I was something that demons were after."

He slammed his palm on the steering wheel before sighing. "Even after witnessing all that, it's still weird to think that demons exist. Killian was the guy back there... What the hell did he turn into?"

We were almost back to Ryan's, leaving the last bit of bumps and grinds as we hit the blacktop of his hollow "He's here to protect me," I said quietly, unsure. So, confused and afraid.

"Protect you," he sounded like he wanted to laugh but it came out in a hiss. He studied my face before saying, "And you believe him?"

"Yeah, I mean," I grumbled and pressed my head into the seat. "He's never not protected me or hurt me. And believe me, he had plenty of chances to." I thought back to all the time I spent with him in my room. And the way he helped me sleep. He saved me from the ghost, Molly, and healed my wound. Guilt smacked me in the face. I just left him there.

"If you believed him, then why did you leave back there?"

I looked down, rubbing my palms against my jeans. "I didn't mean to." That sounded like a lie. "I don't know, I was scared. He changed entirely. You saw him too, what else was I supposed to do?" I asked.

He nodded. "He turned into a skeleton wielding a huge ass scythe that changes into other weapons. I'd say you should stay the hell away from anything like that. But why didn't you tell me, I could have helped."

Helped with what? "Because I didn't want to get you involved. It's dangerous." Now it was too late. He was involved. I could say nothing to change his mind now that he knew.

We pulled into the driveway and I gasped. Killian stood in the driveway waiting. "How does he know where I live?" Ryan asked.

"He knows everything." And that scared me most.

I stepped out of the truck slowly, afraid of what was about to happen. He stepped forward. I couldn't mistake the scowl on his face. But at least he had a face. I placed my hands together trying to calm my shaky nerves. His face softened, only a moment, enough for me to see something there that he meant to hide before turning on Ryan. "I have to erase their memories." Ryan glared, tightening his fists.

I panicked. Erase? "No, Killian. You can't. They won't tell anyone." I reached for his arm and he jerked away like I was venom.

"That's not the problem," Killian hissed. "They are in danger if they know. No, they are in enough danger just by being close to you." His eyes were cold and distance making everything he said hurt more. My friends were in danger just because they were my friends.

"All the more reason we should know," Ryan spoke up, stepping closer. He stared at Killian as if he hadn't just witnessed the things he could do. The monster he can turn in to. "It would be better this way."

Killian looked to be considering what Ryan said. His jaw tightened before softening. "If you were smart, you'd stay away from her." Something about the way he said it... "No, maybe it's best for me to take you out of the human world." He looked back at me and my stomach fluttered with unease.

"You're not taking Melanie anywhere." Ryan sidestepped in front of me, tucking me behind him. Like that would solve anything. Killian would do as he pleased. I nudged Ryan in the shoulder, feeling suffocated.

"When?" I whispered, he looked back at me confused. "Will this awful life ever end for me?" My voice broke and half-cried, half-whispered. "Will I get to be normal? Safe?" He looked away. The answer stung my chest.

I tumbled forward, Ryan caught me in his arms. I caught sight of Killian hurrying to help me up but when Killian reached to take me away, Ryan pulled me closer into his chest. Killian's gaze flickered from Ryan to me, staring at me a moment too long before finally walking away. He moved around the truck and my eyes followed after him. I hadn't noticed how much Ryan's truck suffered until looking at it. I stood up, moving away from Ryan. The hood was caved in a little, both sides were dented, and the hood was scratched up. Killian stood by the truck and magically the truck started returning to normal. The dents came out, the hood, and the paint were fixed in a matter of seconds.

I knew it was the work of Killian's power again, but his hands were in his pockets, his expression blank. Everything looked so easy for him.

Tess banged on the backdoor inside of the truck. Killian opened the door and Tess fell face first into the gravel. I moved my hand to my mouth, gasped, and ran to her. I gave Killian the evil eye before bending down to check on her. He could have caught her. "Are you okay?"

"What happened?" she asked, but then her brown eyes grew wide and terrified. "What about those things?" she mumbled. Before I could answer, Killian covered her eyes with his hand and her face fell into my chest. He picked her up and brought her to Ryan.

"She won't remember anything." Ryan eyed him suspiciously before taking his sister. "You will regret knowing." Killian turned away and I thought he was coming for me. But he didn't. He walked past me and disappeared, once again.

CHAPTER NINE

Tess woke the next morning blissfully unaware of everything that happened the night before. Well, not entirely. She still remembered going to the party and getting drunk, everything went blank from there. Which made me wonder if he even had to wipe her memory, she had been wasted.

I went home that morning, paranoid and afraid. Ryan spent the night trying to comfort me, but I felt distant and confused. Unsure of everything, even my own feelings. I spent Sunday waiting for Killian, but he never came. The cold, dark look in his eyes as he passed me the night before edged my mind. But when night came, I'd doze off and see his skeleton body chasing after me and I'd wake up alone in my room.

The week went by slowly without Killian's presence in my life. The ghosts were still missing at school which meant he was close, just nowhere I could see him. I was always paranoid, everyday walking outside, getting in my car, looking over my shoulder expecting to see a demon.

Somewhere along the time of meeting him I must have believed that he would protect me. I would catch myself looking around for him, whether it was at school or home but mostly at night in my room, where I spent the most time with him. But as the week slipped away slowly—his presence gone—that faith was dwindling. Then I'd remind myself that he wasn't human. That his appearance changed right before my eyes turning him into...

My brain was tired of trying to piece together the puzzle I called my life.

I found myself in the library Friday morning during school. Rarely was there anyone in the library. I found comfort here, surrounded by books. Someone dropped a book over the one I had been reading at my table. I jumped and looked up to see Ryan.

"I knew there was something familiar about his change on Saturday." I hadn't realized Ryan was looking for answers by himself, let alone at all. I avoided the topic every time he brought it up. I studied the book he sat in front of me. It was a new book, brown and hardback. It was called 'Myth and Folklore'.

"What kind of book is this?" I asked.

He shook his head. "Just something on mythical creatures, urban legends, and folklore. It has it all." He opened the book and began flipping through the pages. I saw pictures of wicked creatures and animals that shouldn't exist, but I knew better now. Some were horrifying even on paper. "I found it in the town library yesterday. I stopped after school." Ryan never went to the library. "Here." He stopped on a page.

I grabbed the edges of the book, leaning over it. A skeletal figure was printed on the page, draped with a black cloak and scythe. The drawing was different than Killian's transformation, but it didn't change the fact that everything was the same. It was like looking at a cartoon version of him. I moved my index finger across the paper until I got to the name at the top.

Death; also known as The Grim Reaper.

I could only stare.

This was why it had been so familiar. Everyone's seen a picture depicted of the Grim Reaper at some point. It was obvious to me now. The ghosts feared him. "Death." I whispered, looking up to Ryan.

He nodded. "And I think he's the real deal. Grim fucking Reaper."

———

Ryan followed me home from school. Something he had been doing all week. Now that he knew the danger I was in, I couldn't keep him away. Which honestly, if a demon was to come again what could he do? He was a human. Our strength was nothing compared to the power and strength I'd seen so far.

I helped Mom cook while Ryan played video games with Alex in the living room. I could hear them arguing about something in the distance. "You're upset, wanna talk about?" Mom took notice as she stirred the mashed potatoes. I was removing the homemade biscuits from the oven.

"It's nothing." Nothing she'd understand or believe. It was probably safer that she never believed a word I said as a child.

"Ryan." Mom arched an eyebrow and I groaned. "He's been hanging around all week."

"It's not what you think." Which was the truth, but I knew nothing I could say would change what she believed. No, things were far from romantic between us. Knowing demons were real and after me, Ryan completely changed. The fun and charming friend that I harbored feelings for over the years was missing and replaced with someone that was smothering me like I was a child.

"Oh?" She wasn't convinced.

Mom hollered at the boys to eat. Ryan raced Alex to the table. I smiled, enjoying the fact that he was at least himself in front of my family. "You'd think they were starving." Mom grinned as she spoke. I knew she enjoyed these moments at home with us. So did I. But I knew it was even more enjoyable that I had a boy over. Ryan topped the cake, she adored him so much.

"You've been coming over a lot this week." Alex took a bit of food eyeing Ryan. "Not that I'm complaining." Ryan only smiled and continued eating.

"Your food is always delicious," he praised Mom and she practically swooned.

"So, are you and my sister finally dating?" I choked on a biscuit as Alex waited for an answer. Ryan looked across the table at me, amused.

"Sadly, no. Your sister keeps ignoring all my signals."

I took a sip of Dr. Pepper and tried to ignore what he just said. "Hush, whatever."

"See." He pointed at me with his fork. "She so coldly rejects me." He shook his head staring at Alex.

Mom was glowing. "Now, Melanie."

"You're stupid, sis. Who else would want to date you? I'd be careful about rejecting him," Alex added.

"Alex," Mom hissed.

"You are such a dweeb," I told Alex and he stuck out his tongue.

I helped Mom clean up and Ryan still hadn't left. He even followed me upstairs. Once we were in my room, I shut the door. I turned to face him, practically blowing steam from my ears. "You can stop now."

"Stop what?" He faked ignorance, flopping down on my bed.

"Never leaving my side," I huffed, shaking my head causing stray pieces of blonde hair to fall in my eyes. I tucked them behind my ear.

"It's too dangerous and I don't mind."

"I think you should go." I reopened the door. He sighed and moved off the bed.

"Melanie." I hated the tender way he spoke my name. He looked like he never wanted to leave. Not now, not ever. I knew how he felt because I felt the same way, but my heart just wasn't in it this week. I had a lot going on which was probably why something felt different. Yeah, that was it. "I just want to keep you safe."

"You can't, Ryan." The words left my lips before realizing. It was honest and real, but it wasn't something any guy would want to hear. That they couldn't keep one girl safe. Ryan stumbled back, knowing it was the truth, but unable to accept it. "Please," I whispered. "If you're that worried, you can come back tomorrow." He looked down for a moment. Then walked toward the door, he caught my hand in his. He bent down and kissed my cheek. I looked up, he caught me by surprise.

"I'd do anything to keep you safe." He smiled and walked out the door.

I went to the bed and flopped down. As sweet as Ryan was, the moment he left my sights, my thoughts of him did as well, making me feel guilty. But not for long. Demons plagued my thoughts. The ugly wolf demons. The dead girl called Molly and how she tried to kill me twice. The whatever it had been at the movie theater. Most of all, I thought of Killian. Death. Grim. Reaper. Of all the things that he could have been, being Death was what I would have least expected. It still didn't seem real when I thought about it, I mean come on? But... if Death was a person then Killian had to be him. He was powerful. I now knew why.

Though that wasn't why I thought of him. Every time he crossed my mind—which was a lot—I grew angry and impatience. Where was he? I thought he was protecting me, but he had been gone all week. I knew he didn't need me to see him to keep me safe but...

He pissed me off. I couldn't explain my frustration.

I could call his name again and he might come, but I didn't want to be the one that caved first. So I didn't. I tossed and turned on the bed before pressing my face into a pillow. I screamed and picked my head back up. I looked around my room like I expected him to suddenly be there. I walked to the window and stared outside. I paced. I scribbled furiously in my notebook still expecting him to appear.

The week passed so slowly waiting on him to show up. But he never did. I thought about his other appearance all week and decided I was over it. He was scary, but I reacted badly. I just wanted him to randomly appear like he always had before. Explain everything so that I could understand. Tell me he wasn't some monster. Tell me he was protecting me so that I'd actually feel safe. I wanted him to tell me who he was, not Ryan. Now I probably knew and he hadn't been the one to tell me, which frustrated me.

Couldn't he see how I felt?

Only two weeks, that's the length of time Killian has been in my life and he managed to change everything. The way I felt even seemed different. He was now a part of my life and I hadn't liked it from the very beginning. But now all I felt was...

Lonely. And afraid.

I sat back down on my bed and cradled the pillow.

CHAPTER TEN

I dropped a can of biscuits on my right foot the next morning while making breakfast. I grabbed my foot, hopping around in agony until the pain turned to a dull ache. I found myself in the floor, inspecting the new bruise. This was all Killian's fault. I was so occupied with thoughts of him, wondering where he was that I kept screwing up.

Mom talked me into watching a movie with her, some romantic comedy. I got up and went to my room forty-five minutes in, the male lead was only irritating me. I knew I was a fuse waiting to blow. I slammed my bedroom door. And it was all his fault...

My mood was getting worse. Everything was

driving me crazy just because he was avoiding me! I walked past my full body mirror and stopped, glaring at my reflection. "Don't look at me like that." Yeah, I was going insane, but maybe I was trying to be humorous. Only I wasn't funny.

I was angry. Killian appeared into my life one night and flipped it upside down telling me of demons. That I was some Vessel. And I could have went along with my life just fine, completely unaware of it all if he hadn't stepped in. Ghosts were enough trouble. But after dumping all that crap on me, he goes and what? Disappeared?

Okay… I knew that I was partially… mostly to blame and I'd be dead already if it wasn't for him, but still…

Why me? Why? I was doing a bit self-loathing and 'why, universe, why are you so cruel to me' when Tess barged into my room unexpectedly. "You ready?" She asked like I had a clue what she was talking about.

"I wasn't aware I was going anywhere?" I

frowned.

"Ryan's waiting, hurry!" she snapped. "He wants you to come to his practice." I rolled my eyes, feeling my rage boiling over. He was going overboard.

"I can't. Mom went to the store and I have to stay home with Alex."

Alex must have been in the hallway. "I don't mind going to watch him practice." No, Alex. You weren't supposed to say that, but then he went and gave me puppy dog eyes standing in my doorway. Tess smiled. "I want to get out of the house." He went on.

I sighed. Thirty minutes later, we were on the bleachers watching the team practice on the field. Alex was walking around the track, smiling. Well, it wasn't a total loss. Alex looked happy and was getting exercise. I also noticed him staring at the players with admiration and longing? Did he want to play? Did Mom know?

"Are you dating my brother behind my

back? He's been up your ass all week. More than usual." Tess sat beside me.

"No, of course not," I blubbered. I couldn't tell her the truth.

"That's true. I would be the first to know." She smiled and I felt the guilt eating me alive. She didn't know anything; she could be in danger just sitting next to me.

I was horrible.

Ryan waved at us from the field, but I turned my head away. They practiced a few plays and I continuously sighed. The wind blew with a heavy chill. I covered my arms. That was right. It was October now, warm days were dwindling, maybe but a few were left before the cold settled in for good.

"Mike looks so sexy when he's all sweaty and filthy." I smiled and touched my lips for a moment. How nice to be normal and guy problems being the biggest issue.

"How are you two?" I attempted at a

conversation.

She started grinning and I knew that look well. "We finally had sex last night." It was surprising that it took this long, Tess wasn't one to shy away from sexual encounters. She never denied any of her past either. She accepted who she was. I wished I had her confidence.

"Well, how was it?" I asked not having the slightest bit of experience myself, but with reading came knowledge. Or at least I hoped. But experience was probably more so?

"Good," she chirped smiling at Mike on the field. "The best so far, I'm not even lying Melanie." I ignored the 'so far' comment wondering if that meant that she didn't think her and Mike would last.

"I'm happy for you." And I meant it, but I was envious all the same. I wanted a taste of normal, but normal didn't want a thing to do with me.

Practice ended and the boys scattered off the

field. Ryan went to Alex and they walked together. Ryan rubbed his head as they laughed about something. After that, Ryan took us to Pizza Hut. Alex was enjoying himself and that almost put me in a better mood. I caught Ryan staring at me a lot as we ate, he must want to tell me something. We hadn't spoken to each other all day, I guess he figured I was upset with him. Tess left with Mike after we ate and Ryan drove us home.

Mom was asleep in her room; it would be time for her to leave for work soon. Ryan followed us in.

"Thanks for the food," Alex told him before kicking off his shoes and running upstairs to his room. Now, we were alone. The tension was heavy between us.

"You're upset with me." I watched him hesitate. "Why?" He tried to pull me close, but I shoved him away.

"Ryan, I can't handle you hovering over me. You haven't left my side all week!"

"I'm worried about you." He dropped his head down.

"I know; I understand that but I think..." The words felt like sand in my mouth, being forced to come out. "I think we should keep a distance between us, only for now. Stop contact between each other besides school. I can't risk your life."

"You can't be serious." He reached for my hands. Our fingers slid against each other before I pulled away. "What about you?" His voice was full of hurt and anger. "Who's going to protect you?" He clenched his fist.

"Killian." His name fell from my tongue so quickly that I knew I believed it. There also came peace with realizing that. I believed him. That's why I was still waiting.

"He turned into a monster right in front of us." Ryan's face was red with anger. "Have you even seen him since then?"

I looked away. "No."

"How can you trust him. He's not like us.

He's not human." Ryan was bitter, tossing his head up and back down in aggravation.

But I kept my eyes focused on his. "He's never hurt me."

He wasn't convinced. "You know nothing about him."

"Lower your voice," I hushed him, afraid of waking Mom. I hated that we were being so angry with each other. It wasn't like us at all.

"He hasn't been around to protect you all week." He was though. "Some protector," Ryan muttered. I wanted to smack him for being so childish. Then I realized this wasn't about being safe at all. Was this jealousy?

My expression hardened. "I'm not arguing. Go." I turned to the front door and opened it.

Ryan's anger faded, shoulders slumped in defeat. He looked sad and maybe even afraid. "Don't make me leave when it's like this between us." His voice was soft and I knew he was back to being levelheaded.

But our emotions had already gotten the best of us. "You're the one that's making it like this," I hissed trying to keep my tiny voice. If I didn't hurry, my emotions were going to be spilling out of my eyes. "Do you ever stop to think about how I would feel if something were to happen to you because of me?" My voice broke, but my eyes never left his.

He pushed anyway. "What about me?" He stepped closer until his face was over mine and grabbed my cheeks. I took that moment to close my eyes and remember the way this felt, having him so close. If only for a moment. If things had been different, if I was normal, this would be the moment his lips finally met mine. But that wasn't my reality. I opened my eyes. "How can I sit back and do nothing when the girl I love--"

I jerked away so abruptly he didn't get a chance to finish. "Don't."

This time, I knew I hurt him. I watched his expression harden with resolve. "I won't sit back and do nothing." He wasn't lying which was the worst part of all.

"Go, Ryan" I pointed toward the door. Before leaving, he leaned over and tucked a piece of hair behind my ear. A kind gesture before stepping out the door.

I shut the door in a hurry. I gripped the doorknobs, tears escaping the prison they were locked in. I moved away from the door afraid he might hear me. My tears turned to loud sobs as I went to the kitchen. I grabbed a glass from the cabinet and poured some milk into it. My lips trembled as the glass touched my lips. I whimpered while trying to take a drink causing the milk to run down my chin. Somehow, I was covered in it. Probably wasn't a good idea to drink something while crying. I moved to the sink and began to clean up the spilled milk on my chin and chest. It was dark out so when I stared out the window all I saw was my own reflection staring back at me. Blonde, wavy hair fell over my shoulders that needed to be washed. My eyes were puffy and red, so were my face and neck.

Seeing how pitiful I looked only made me feel worse. I stepped away from the sink and stopped. I thought I saw something move, only nothing was there. I shook my head and walked into the kitchen. I noticed it again. I looked at the wall and saw the reflection of my shadow. Now I was terrified of my own shadow, I rolled my eyes. I wiped underneath my eyes, feeling somewhat refreshed after crying. It was good to let it all out but now I had a raging headache.

I walked to the stairs, stopping once again. I looked behind me, puzzled. Hmm. I could have sworn my shadow was on the wall, how was it behind me? I was being a moron. Shadows changed with the direction I moved and the lighting. I hovered my feet over the next step... Then again, something hadn't been right.

I lost my footing and fell forward catching myself with my hands. "Oaf!" escaped my lips from the impact and pinpricks ran up my arms from the awkward way I fell. I sighed, flipping my hair out of my face and turning back to see my own shadow standing over me.

What the...? Another demon? No time to stare.

I tried to stand up, but my legs weren't moving. I looked back and saw that the shadow had my ankle in its hand. I felt the slight pull before being dragged down the stairs. I reached out to hold onto something, but there was nothing. My stomach and chest bounced off the steps and I finally got a grip on the banister. The shadow jerked harder and I lost my grip, causing me to miss the rest of the steps and land on the floor. The shadow flipped me onto my back. I grunted and fought back, but it was like fighting air. "Stop! Get away from me," I yelled.

This was bad. If I didn't do something... I was in danger of dying. AGAIN.

The shadow stopped fighting me. It hovered

above me. All it took was a second and the shadow jumped through me. No, my stomach knotted. It was inside me. I was present in my own mind, but not my body. I watched through my own eyes as I stood up and started walking to the kitchen. I tried talking, but no words came out. I lost control of every part of myself.

Where was Killian? Hasn't he noticed yet? Surely, he could sense I was in danger, right? What if... he really stopped protecting me? I was so sure he would be there. Maybe Ryan had been right? I was foolish to put trust in someone that wasn't human. My panic grew as my body went to the counter and grabbed a kitchen knife.

This was it, I was going to die and there was nothing I could do about it.

Killian. I whispered his name in my mind. The shadow—Me grabbed the biggest knife we had. The light reflected off the clean blade as I brought it above my chest with both arms. It was at that moment I realized that I couldn't always be saved. Yet, I didn't want to die. I couldn't die, not like this. My desperation crawled through me. No matter how screwed up my life was, I didn't want it to end. So, I had to find my own way.

This was my body, my body, my body! My mind was clear; my reason was strong. I saw the knife shake in my hand. I could feel the shadow inside me, an invisible yet strong force. One that didn't belong. It was a darkness that rested against my control and I couldn't shake it off. I started to push at it. I could feel the strain, the tug and pull, the inner battle within myself that couldn't be seen, only felt.

The knife aimed at my chest began to move and I used all my strength to fight against it. The shadow pulled halfway out of my body with a strange winding noise as it did. "OMIGOD, Melanie!" Mom's high pitched scream broke my concentration for a moment, but I blocked it out. I closed my eyes, realizing I gained some control as the shadow was forced out of my body more.

Not soon enough, the knife was already in motion. I couldn't stop it so I forced it to move just in time cutting into my shoulder. I screamed as the knife pierced my skin and went through to the bone. Mom shocked and horrified, said things to me I couldn't understand.

I felt my willpower and energy leave me as the shadow was almost all the way back inside me. I used what strength I had left to call his name. "Killian." He was there before I finished saying it. His eyes caught on, growing dangerously dark as he noticed the knife embedded in my shoulder. He looked frightening, I'd never seen him look so scary as he strode toward me. I lost control over my body and I couldn't tell him about the shadow so I could only hope he knew. And he didn't disappoint me. His hand went inside my chest and my whole body jerked. He pulled the shadow out, but the shadow latched onto me trying to go back inside. Its effort was futile against Killian. With a bit more pull from Killian, the shadow ripped away from me. I gasped for air, dropping my hand from the knife embedded in my shoulder. My whole body shook from the pain I was in. My shirt was covered in blood and so were my hands. Mom's sobbing broke through my rattled mind and I looked up to see her staring at me, horror and fear filled her expression. Her eyes bounced from me to Killian as he disposed of the shadow.

After destroying it, he ran to my side. I shook my head, clenching hard against my teeth. "What?" Mom eyes were wild and unrecognizable. "Why did you try to," she broke in loud sobs again as she brought her hand over her mouth. She looked terrified. I fell against the counter feeling dizzy. Killian hurried to hold me up. I pushed him away slightly.

"Please." I looked up to meet his eyes. "My mom. Do something, she's freaking out," I pleaded.

"I will, but first let me take the knife out."

I grabbed his hand. "Please." My mom was

barely keeping it together. No, she was already lost in what she thought she saw. I couldn't stand seeing her like that. Most of all, I couldn't stand the look she gave me when I stabbed myself. She couldn't have known that it wasn't me, but a part of her found it so easy to believe that I could hurt myself. The fear in her eyes had been because of me. And that hurt more than any physical pain.

He nodded, understanding my feelings and went to her. She backed away from him shrieking and terrified. His hand moved to her head quickly and she fell backwards. He caught her and gently laid her down in the floor. He hurried back to me.

With Mom taken care of I was finally able to notice my whole body shaking from the pain. I whimpered as I slid down the counter onto the floor. He bent down next to me and I shook my head. I cried out when his hand moved toward the knife in my shoulder. "I need to take it out." He told me gently.

"It's gonna hurt. I can't handle any more

pain," I cried. My pain tolerance was low, but now that the danger was gone, I couldn't handle it.

He pressed his finger and thumb underneath my chin and raised my head so that I was looking at him. "It's not gonna hurt," he promised.

I nodded, calming my tears and closing my eyes. I felt the weight of his hand touch the knife and tensed. The pain numbed instantly. I opened my eyes as he jerked the knife out. Blood gushed at a faster pace, and Killian cupped the wound quickly. I saw the light and the flow of his power healing me. When he removed his hand, I was healed. I sagged in relief against the counter.

The kitchen was a bloody mess. My blood. It covered the floor around me. My shirt was covered and so were Killian's hands. I saw Mom's feet poking out around the corner of the bar in the middle of the kitchen and knew I needed to get her in bed before her alarm went off for work. I also needed to clean the mess. I started to get up and Killian grabbed my arms to help me up. I was too exhausted to shrug him off.

He went to the sink and washed his hands. "Go wash yourself up. I'll get rid of the mess," he told me with his back turned toward the sink.

"My mom."

"I'll carry her to bed," he added softly. I went upstairs and peeked in Alex's room. He was sitting in front of the TV with a pair of headphones on. From this distance, I could hear the headphones perfectly. It was a good thing he couldn't hear anything. I shut his door. He continued his game unaware of what happened downstairs.

I showered and scrubbed the blood off. I stood there with the water pouring over me until my skin tingled and turned red from the scalding temperature of the water. I slipped on a baggy shirt and loose shorts and bagged up the clothes that I had been wearing. I went back downstairs with the bag and tossed it in the trash. The kitchen was clean. Not a drop of blood left on the floor. He used his power again. I hurried to Mom's room and quietly opened the door. She was sleeping. I sighed and went to my room

Killian was there waiting on me. I went inside and shut my bedroom door behind me. He sat on my bed, shoulders slumped in defeat. My entire being fluttered in his presence. I grabbed my chest, willed myself to remember the past week. I was tired and upset, somehow I didn't want to have this conversation tonight. All the time spent waiting on him. All the questions I had suddenly felt like a barrier between us.

Right now, I just wanted to crawl under my cover and hide. *I almost died. Where were you?* Then I felt foolish for even caring so much.

"You can go now; I'd like to get some rest." I stood awkwardly at the door. I was almost positive that nothing could prevent me from falling asleep the moment my head hit the pillow—even my own thoughts and worries.

"I'm staying." He finally picked his head up.

"You can rest, though." He stood up and the distance didn't matter, he was freakishly tall and imposing. He only felt even more so when we were alone. Why did he have to be so big and manly making me feel so... small? He stepped closer before bringing his hand out to trace the curve of my neck. A shiver ran through me. It wasn't bad, but it wasn't comfortable either. It was different. A new feeling. I inhaled sharply before sliding to the side and away from him. His eyes followed me—always. Like I was something to study and learn, every part of me, everything I did. I felt like he calculated everything.

"There's no way I'd be able to fall asleep if you're here." That was a lie. The safest I felt all week was right here with him. I couldn't deny that he made me feel safe. Which also made it the most exhausting moment as well. But my body burned with anger when I thought about how safe I felt right now and how I waited for him all week. He managed to both calm and annoy me. "Why bother protecting me now? You haven't all week, why start again?" I crossed my arms over my chest. I knew I was acting childish, but I couldn't stop my actions.

He sighed. "You're right. It's seems I'm only ever healing you instead of protecting you." I wasn't expecting him to agree so easily. I looked down. "But I've never left your side, Melanie. I would never go so far away to put you—"

"Then what about what just happened?" I glared, raising up my head and meeting his dark pooled eyes. "Just a moment longer I would have been," my voice wavered and I couldn't hold my eyes with his any longer. "It was hard. Fighting against something inside your own body, looking out but unable to do anything. It was frightening and I couldn't fight that control any longer."

He took my hand while I was distracted. He gave it a gentle squeeze. "That will never happen again. I would have detected any other demonic attack but shadows are different. They have no presence. I hadn't expected him to use one, which was foolish on my part." He hesitated. "I'm thinking it would be best to stay by your side all the time." His voice was different, deeper and husky. Which was strange, the room was strange. I was thinking strange things. The small lamp on my nightstand cast a glow over his features. I simply looked at him. And the more I did, I wondered what part of me had found him displeasing to the eyes? Okay, he did look scary, but not so much anymore. More like mysterious. I'd admit, he was truly handsome. Rugged and chiseled to what I'd consider perfection.

"You must hate that," I whispered feeling a tad shy. How random but yeah, that was me. "I know how much it displeases you to protect this *Human,*" I mocked his tone.

I didn't miss the smile that tugged at his lips. I had never seen him smile like that. Sure, I had seen his cocky, know-it-all smiles, but nothing as real as this one. He laughed slowly before saying,

"Oh, Melanie." He moved the hand that was holding mine and brought it up to my cheek. He lazily rubbed his thumb across it. "If I'm not mistaken, it sounds like you've missed me a great deal despite pretending otherwise." I forgot how to breathe with the playful way he spoke. "I didn't come around this week, not because I didn't want to. I thought you were afraid of me after you saw what I was." His hand left my cheek, dropping at his side. His smile was sad and forced as he looked at me.

I moved past him quickly sucking air back into my lungs. "I'm not afraid." Then stopped walking and sighed. "Okay, that was a lie. You scared the crap out of me last week. But that's only normal considering you turned into a skeleton figure that wielded a giant weapon. I mean, really." I turned back around and went back to face him puffing out my cheeks. "Would it have been so hard to say, 'oh hey, I turn into walking bones sometimes' or something." I lifted my arms in frustration. "So, yes I *was* afraid. You were super scary that night and I was still shaken up afterwards when I reacted coldly toward you. But I've had all week to think about whether I'm afraid of you." I took a deep breath and looked at him. "No, I'm not afraid of you." Mostly.

Killian looked unsure, but his smiled seemed more genuine than before. Then I remembered something important. "This is probably gonna sound insane, but you wouldn't happen to be the Grim Reaper?" I lifted my eyebrows with half a smile as I waited for his answer.

"You finally figured it out?" He scratched his chin, looking up. "Yeah, I am."

My jaw dropped. Thinking he was and *knowing* he was Grim Reaper were entirely different things. "Really?"

Something wicked flashed in the depth of his eyes before his lip curved into a smile. "Not every day you get to meet Death in the flesh." He held out his arms and I snorted. Was he always so vain? "Did you just snort at Death, Melanie?" his voice grew dark and dangerous. I shivered. The feeling of constantly being afraid and feeling safe around him always left me confused.

"N-no," I stumbled with the word. "I just find it hard to believe that Grim Reaper would be protecting me. You said so from the beginning yourself," I added.

He sighed. "I did. It was a request. From Heaven."

"Heaven?" I let the word sink in and looked to him in disbelief. Heaven wanted me safe?

"Yes, need I remind you that you're a dangerous weapon in the hands of a demon. Heaven can't allow that to ever happen."

"Right," I muttered. "How can I forget with all these demons after me?" I added with venom. But that also made me think of another thing I wanted to ask. "Killian-Grim." I held up my hand. "Whoever. There's something I'd like to ask."

He nodded for me to continue. "When my dad passed... there was a cloaked figure standing next to him seconds before he," I coughed, straightening out my voice. "Was that you?"

He studied me a moment before replying quickly, "No." I frowned. "I am Grim Reaper, but I have many other Reaper's that do my job for me. I would never get a moment to myself if I tended to every dying person." I nodded understanding, but I couldn't help feeling disappointed.

"So, what do you do exactly?" I asked, fiddling with the bottom of my shirt. "Send the dead to the afterlife?"

He went to my bed and sat down, running his hand through his hair. A habit I caught him doing a lot. He placed his elbows on his knees and looked up. That was when I noticed my legs were sore from standing and joined him on the bed. I placed one leg underneath my butt and turned around to face him. "I send the dead to Heaven or Hell. If they were kind and good people, honest for most of their life; they ascend to Heaven. The ones that are evil and corrupted, they descend to Hell. I'm the middle, I make sure they get where they need to go."

I nodded. "What about the ghosts? Why aren't they leaving?"

"They hide from Reapers. Ghosts are still attached to something in the living that causes them to run from the afterlife. Love, hate, anger, jealousy, revenge. Any emotion can turn into a weapon against them if it's strong enough that keeps them with the living."

"That makes sense. There's this boy I know that has an ancestor following him around. She's always judging girls that get close to him. She's so grumpy." I shook my head thinking about her and he laughed.

"Sounds like her reason for staying was love. She wanted to watch over her family."

I grinned. "Yeah, I figured as much. Still, she's got a mean mouth on her." He never stopped smiling as I spoke which made me think that he might enjoy listening to what I said. Ryan listened to me. Tess occasionally did when I talked about ghosts. But neither could understand my world. Not like Killian. "So, about this demon that is after me."

He stopped smiling as if remembering his whole reason for being here. "You ask a lot of questions for someone that was almost killed." I shuddered thinking about the pain I felt when I was stabbed.

"I'm just tired of not knowing anything."

"Tomorrow. Let's talk about everything. Tonight, you should rest." He patted the bed and gestured for me to lay down.

I yawned. I was tired. I was only ignoring it because he was finally here. "Yeah, I am sleepy." I admitted and slipped into the covers. I turned around to face him once I was underneath. I scooted the pillow closer to where he sat.

"Do you need me to help you sleep?" he

whispered softly, touching my forehead.

I shook my head and a grin spread across my face. "No, I think I'm good." The smile told me he liked my answer. "Are you staying?" I looked up from the pillow at him.

"Yeah."

"Don't you sleep?"

He laughed. "I'm insanely powerful."

I rolled my eyes. "You're so vain," I told him.

"You didn't let me finish." He moved closer. "I'm powerful, but I still require some sleep but nowhere near as much as humans." I closed my eyes and listened as he spoke.

"Oh?" I whispered drowsily. "You should sleep then."

I heard him laugh again before I drifted asleep.

CHAPTER ELEVEN

When I woke, Killian was gone. I stared up at the ceiling as I thought about last night. I had *almost* died a lot lately, but Killian was back at least. Mom had witnessed everything. I closed my eyes trying to block out the images of the way she looked at me. At least she wouldn't remember. But I would.

I found myself disappointed that Killian wasn't here. I thought he wasn't going to leave my side? I climbed out of bed, shaking my head, not liking the directions my thoughts were taking me. It was doing that a lot lately. Thinking about him and wondering where he was. I shouldn't care as much as I did.

There was a knock on the door downstairs. I

heard Alex yell for Mom to answer it. One of them opened the door. The voices were low and I couldn't make out anything else. I shrugged my shoulders. It was probably Ryan. With the way we left things last night I was surprised he would come today. Ryan wasn't someone to give up. That meant that I would end up having to say the same mean things over again. I changed out of my pajamas.

How much danger were Mom and Alex in because of me? I couldn't avoid them like I did Ryan. I needed to ask Killian when I saw him again. I couldn't stand the thought of something happening to them. "Melanie, get down here! You have a visitor," Mom yelled. I arched my brow. That was strange. If Ryan or Tess was at the door Mom would have just told them to go upstairs to get me. Which meant someone else was at the door.

It wouldn't be some sort of demon, would it? Feeling worried, I rushed downstairs and stopped when I reached the bottom step. Killian stood next to Mom in the doorway. I gave him a confused look. He simply smiled. What was he up to? "Melanie," he said my name with an alarming amount of charm and eagerness. He glowed with happiness. It was too unnatural. I realized he was putting on an act in front of Mom. Why was he trying so hard? I didn't want to tell him how forced his acting looked, so I walked to where they stood.

"What are you doing here?" I asked slowly, feeling Mom's gaze burning a hole through me. She studied Killian with caution and uncertainty. I could already tell that she was disapproving everything about him.

"You know this *man?*" I didn't miss the way she called him 'man', implying that she knew he wasn't my age, nor did he go to my school. He was older.

"Yeah," I answered trying to come up with a better answer. "He's a friend of Ryan's," I added. I knew it was a mistake the moment the words left my mouth, but it was too late to change my answer.

She eyed him, her piercing gaze studying him top to bottom. I wanted to hide my eyes from the way she was acting. "Ryan's friend?" She didn't sound convinced. "Then why is he here?" She crossed her arms against her chest.

"Mom," I hissed, not being able to handle any more embarrassment. I knew she probably thought we were in some sort of relationship. Of course, it would look like that. Still, she should know her daughter enough to know that she didn't date. Ever.

Killian coughed, interrupting us. I looked up. "My name's Killian. It's a pleasure to meet you." I held back the eye roll. Look at him acting like a gentleman.

"Strange name." Mom didn't bother to introduce herself. Her behavior was surprising; she was well on manners. She never treated anyone so coldly. Although, I figured it might have something to do with Killian's age. I didn't know how old he was either, but it was clear that he was older than me. Not that he looked very friendly either, even when he smiled.

"So I've heard."

"Let's go talk outside." I moved quickly, passing Mom and grabbing his shoulder. I jerked him backward out the door with me. I heard Mom's aggravated blow as I shut the door. I knew I would be answering questions later. I stepped off the porch knowing she was probably going to try to spy out the window. I tiptoed barefoot on the walkway until my feet hit the gravel driveway. I let go of his arm and glared. "What in the world are you doing?"

He shrugged his shoulders and went to lean against my car. "I figured it make things easier if your mom met me."

I rubbed my head before saying, "Does that even make sense? You have all that power; you don't have to ever worry about her seeing you. And besides, look at you." I pointed at him. "You look about ten years older than me. How old are you anyway, twenty-eight? Twenty-seven?" I was actually curious and wanted to know more about him.

"That depends." He crossed his arms and placed his muscular arm across his chest. "Are we talking human years or demon?"

I squinted my eyes. "Does it matter?"

"Yes. Time moves a lot slower where you live. So, if you meant human years, then about three hundred." My mouth dropped. "But if we go by my actual age then three thousand." He said it so casually as if it weren't a big deal.

"Are you serious?"

"Does it look like I'm joking?" he replied then a huge grin spread across his face.

I shook my head. "You're ancient."

"I'm still young," he disagreed.

"If you say so," I muttered. I leaned against the car beside him.

"What are you doing today?" he asked.

I sighed. "Well, I'll probably be interrogated once I go back inside. She will be wondering how I know someone who's much older than me. A lot older," I added. "I've never seen her act that way toward anyone before."

He looked over, scrunching his eyebrows at me. "You're just used to her fawning over Ryan."

"She does not."

He went on, "She does. She adores him." The way he was looking at me… I had to turn away. "She wants the two of you together," he stated.

"Yeah, most likely," I admitted. He looked up at the sky.

"You want to be with him also." He knew my feelings for Ryan. Although I wasn't sure of the confusion I felt lately. Toward Ryan—Toward him.

"But it's pointless. I can't ever be with him. My life is so screwed up." I shrugged while kicking the gravel.

"He doesn't care about that."

"It doesn't matter. I will not allow him to get hurt or worse, killed because of me," I added grouchily and it made him smile. "What about my mom and Alex? Are they in danger because of me?"

He moved away from the car. "Yeah." I felt my heart sink. I knew the answer already, but I had also been hoping for a miracle. I felt the tightening of my throat. "He is growing impatient. He hasn't even tried going after you full force. Your family and friends are all tools he can use against you."

"I can't let that happen, Killian." I shook my head.

"Yeah, I thought so." He nodded. "Meet me at that tiny diner in town...what's it called?" He looked to me for the answer.

"Deb's?"

"Be there in an hour," he said before walking off.

"Wait," I tried to call after him, but his habit of disappearing in thin air left me alone. I looked to the house and hoped Mom wasn't peeking out the window when he vanished. She was waiting for me in the kitchen when I went inside. I tried to make a run for my room, but she stopped me.

"Not so fast, Melanie." I sighed, turning around to go in to the kitchen.

"He's not my boyfriend," I said as soon as I entered the room.

She frowned and crossed her arms. She was sitting on one of the bar stools. "Then what was he doing here?"

"He's a friend of Ryan's. Can't I be friends with him?" I moved my hands in the air and asked.

She sighed. "He looks older. How much older is he?" Her nose scrunched up every time she was irritated or annoyed. Like right now.

"I'm not sure." I looked away. My lies were piling up.

"Melanie," her voice held warning.

"What?" I frowned.

"He looks dangerous; I don't want him

around."

"Mom, you don't even know him!" I grumbled. Although he was Grim Reaper. I had seen just how dangerous he could be.

"I don't want to know him and neither will you!"

"I'm eighteen now, remember?"

"You live under my roof."

The phone rang and I moved to get it off the bar before she could. It was Ryan's house. Whether it was him or Tess, I didn't know.

"It's Tess or Ryan," I told her before she decided to take the phone from my hand. I walked upstairs with the phone. I pressed the end button pretending that I was answering the phone. "Hello?" I paused a moment before speaking again as I climbed the stairs. "Hey, Ryan." I kept the pretend conversation going until I was in my room and sure she couldn't hear me anymore. I tossed the phone down on the bed with a sigh. It was probably Ryan who called and I just wasn't ready to talk to him yet. I felt guilty for lying so much to Mom, but she didn't know anything.

I changed clothes and waited around forty-five minutes before going back downstairs. I grabbed my keys off the kitchen counter. Mom found me as I was slipping on my shoes. "Where are you going?" she asked.

"To the library. I have nothing to read." And I told myself I would go to the library afterwards so that I wouldn't be lying.

She nodded, deciding to believe me. "Be careful. We're supposed to get some bad storms rolling in this evening."

"I will."

Deb's Diner was always crowded on Saturday's. I walked in and found Killian right away despite the huge crowd. Deb's was a nice place. Tess and I stopped here a lot whenever I had the extra money. The walls were gray, but everything else was red or black. The booths were black with sparkly red cushions. Black stools with red seats. Deb loved her retro look, but it never took away the homey feel to the place. Everyone in town loved coming here. Family, friends, people of all ages. Deb's husband, Bob, was one of the cooks and his food was always amazing. Deb took care of the front work. They also had a few waitresses and waiters. She smiled and waved when she saw me walk in. I smiled back and walked to the booth where Killian sat.

He chose the back booth in the corner. He leaned back against the cushion seats. His legs looked cramped underneath the table and he gave off that vibe that made people think twice before approaching him. I slid into the booth, the seat facing him. He grunted and tried to shift his legs underneath the table so that I could squeeze mine in. "It's okay. My legs are tiny compared to your long ones." He tilted his head and studied me. "What?" I frowned.

"Your lips are red." I looked away and grabbed one of the menus next to the salt and pepper. I used the menu to cover my face. I felt the flame in my cheeks rising and didn't want him to see. Why did I wear lipstick? I never wore makeup. I was an idiot.

"It's lipstick," I said still hiding my face behind the menu.

He snorted. "I know what lipstick is."

"Melanie. It's good to see you." Deb stood next to our table. I smiled as I dropped my menu down. She kept her hair dyed black and wore her makeup just as dark despite her age. She enjoyed looking nice, I supposed.

"Hi Deb."

"I haven't seen you around lately. How's my favorite twins? Where are they hiding themselves?" she asked.

"Ryan stays busy with football and Tess has a boyfriend."

"That girl, another one?" She grinned.

I laughed. "I think she really likes this one."

"Oh?" Deb sounded surprised and Killian

cleared his throat. Deb turned to look at him. He propped his elbow on the table, looking at me. "And who is this?" Deb arched her eyebrow. "Don't believe I've seen you before and I think I'd remember if I have."

"Killian." He nodded his head slightly. "I'm a friend of Melanie's."

Deb had a gleam in her eye as she looked back to me. "Is that so?" she said curiously. "Just friends."

"Yeah," I added quickly and stuck my nose back into the menu.

"I'd reckon Ryan would be quite heartbroken if you were to find a man." This woman, I closed my eyes and took a silent but deep breath. She never held her tongue. I peeked over the menu and saw that Killian had gone still. His hands rested together in front of his face. His knuckles looked white he was gripping them so hard. Deb must have sensed his mood. "What can I get you two to drink?"

"Coke."

"Same."

"Do you y'all know what you want?" She looked back and forth between us.

"I'll take the usual. Cheeseburger and fries." She nodded.

"The same," he said again. He never once opened his menu. When she walked away, I frowned at him.

"Don't you eat?"

"Yes." He moved his elbows off the table. He scanned the diner. "I'm not a vampire." His mood was strange ever since Deb brought up Ryan.

"Okay," I replied sharply. "You didn't even look at the menu."

"I don't mind what I eat. I'm not as picky as—"

"Humans," I used his monotone and stuck at my tongue. He finally smiled and I felt the tension ease. "Got it." I placed the menu down. "Why did you ask to meet here? It's not exactly a place to have the sort of conversation I thought we were going to have." Deb came back with our drinks. She placed them on the table.

"Your food will be out in a minute."

"Okay." I smiled as she sped away to another table.

"I thought you'd be hungry." It sounded like he was avoiding the question.

"I am, but that's not what I'm asking."

"You seem close with the woman." He nodded his head toward Deb.

"Yeah, I've been coming to this diner all my life."

Deb brought our food. Killian ate food quicker than anyone I had seen. He scarfed it down. I still had half my food left as he crammed the last bite of his burger in his mouth. "Are you sure you're not the one who's hungry?" He tossed the straw from his cup and downed his Coke. He smiled and sat the empty cup down.

"When I use power, Melanie, I must

replenish. Like humans need food and sleep to survive, so do I and most demons. Just our needs could be entirely different or the same. I could go without sleep or food a lot longer than you, but it will eventually take its toll on me. Especially when I use any sort of power or become Grim. It's draining."

"Really? Hmm, with all that power I figured you—" I let the words die out when I saw the look on his face.

"Will you question everything?" he muttered.

"Probably," I admitted.

I finished my food and leaned back patting my stomach. "I'm so full."

He tossed money on the table and I blinked several times at the outrageous tip. "Is there any where you'd like to go?" he asked standing up. Why was he acting so strange? I could only stare as he grabbed my arm and pulled me out of the booth. He never let go as he led us outside. I let him lead, not understanding him or even myself. I remembered the first time he grabbed my hand. It had been in the parking lot at Ryan's football game. Now I felt the same thing again. I studied our hands. It felt like I was missing a puzzle piece in my head. I tilted my head, just what was this?

"What are you doing?" I asked.

"Do you trust me?" What kind of question was that? I finally looked away from our fingers entwined and searched his face. I couldn't handle his intense gaze more than a couple of seconds and had to look back to our hands. Even his hands were much longer than mine. Before I started rationalizing everything, I nodded and looked back up. He smiled. He led us around the corner of Deb's until we were in the back—away from watchful eyes. There was a dumpster beside the back door. A small cliff was the only thing back here.

"Why did you bring us back here?" I looked to him confused.

"I want to show you what I am."

"But I've already seen who you are," I told him already getting nervous.

"You've seen me, but you don't know what I do." He added, "Let me show you." He gripped my hand, but my smile dropped. The thought of seeing him as Grim scared me. He saw my fear and let go. The moment he did I wanted to reach out and make that connection between us again.

"I would never hurt you," he said softly. I believed him.

"You just seemed like a different person that night."

"It's not that I'm different, Melanie, it's just I'm most powerful in that form. It doesn't change who I am. I'm me but different. I'm Grim." That made no sense to me, but I knew nothing about his world. "Aren't you curious? I'm offering to show you." He offered his hand out. It reached between us. I stared at his palm. Why did taking his hand suddenly seem like so much more? I looked up already knowing my choice. I stepped closer and placed my hand in his. His fingers closed around my hand. A grin spread across his face. "No going back now." I lost my breath at that smile. I didn't care what happened next.

Everything went dark around us. Dark then light as I realized a little too late that he was using his power to take us somewhere. When the light finally faded, I was falling from the sky. I screamed. Grass and trees rapidly drew closer below me. My stomach was in my throat as I continued screaming. I could see my death getting closer and closer with every breath I took. I closed my eyes and waited for the moment my body would hit the large tree branches. Something grabbed my ankle and I stopped falling. The blood rushed to my head and a laugh erupted above me. Grim floated above me with a tight grip on my ankle.

"OMIGOD!" I screamed. "What are you doing?" He shook his head and laughed even more. The laugh caused a shiver to run up my spine. It was Killian's voice, only thundering of power and mischief. He flung me up in the air above him and caught me in his arms. I would have pushed the lunatic away if we hadn't been dangling in the sky.

"Hold tight," his voice danced in my ear. I wrapped my arms around his waist. His waist was a lot smaller as Grim. There was no bulk of muscles, only the cool touch of bones through his shirt. I screamed my heart out as he dropped us down from the sky, through the trees. The moment we were on land, I pushed myself out of his arms. I didn't have enough balance, though and it caused me to fall on my butt. I stood and dusted myself off. I glared at him.

"Are you crazy?" I asked him. Then my frown faded as I took in our surroundings. The trees were monstrous. Well, just not what I was used to seeing. It was dark, but this place was beautiful. Everything was so green, wet, and dewy. Vines wrapped around the trees. Moss covered the ground and a tiny river flowed between my feet. It looked like a tropical forest. "Where in the world did you take me?" I asked Grim.

He looked around, scratching his chin before shrugging his shoulders. He didn't even know? I tossed my hands in the air. "Are you serious? Get us out of here," I yelled. Then I heard a noise. I could hear some sort of bug chirping, but it went quiet. I couldn't make out any of the sounds, my imagination was beginning to run wild. It sounded somewhere between a monkey and a laugh. I rubbed my sweaty palms against my jeans. "What was that?" I whispered.

Instead of answering, he grabbed my wrist and pulled me forward. He took me through a path. We walked over several huge tree roots and followed along the tiny river until a lake came into view. I continued walking forward after he released my arm. It was beautiful. Clear and blue. The moonlight bounced off the water and lit up the trees around the lake. I bent down and scooped the water in my palms. It was warm.

Movement in the middle of the lake caused me to look up. Ripples started from the middle, spreading across the lake. A large tentacle darted out from the water and latched onto my arm, pulling me forward. Grim was there before it could and tossed me backward. He moved in front of me, putting himself between me and the water. And whatever was in it. "Water demon," he answered my unspoken question as he studied the water.

Bubbles rapidly popped in the middle and a woman rose out of them. She was stunning. Red hair, green eyes, and scaly skins. Then I saw the rest of her body. The lower half of her body were tentacles. Green and slimy looking, like an octopus.

"Grim, what brings you here?" She smiled at him with wander and glee.

"Pearl," he answered by reaching out his hand.

"You want my one and only pearl?" she

laughed and he nodded. "I'm afraid I can't do that. But, what did you bring? Smells delicious." She sniffed the air and licked her lips, her eyes landing on me. I took a step back.

"Nothing of your concern. Tonight, you die." Her smile faded and her eyes narrowed. A tentacle shot out of the water toward Grim. His scythe appeared and sliced it in half. She screamed. "You bring a human with you, disgracing me and all demons, and ask for my pearl!" she growled.

"My scythe demands your life, demon," Grim spoke with a thunderous command. "All the humans you ate, the souls you trapped, I demand their release." His scythe turned into a spear. She hissed at the weapon. "Your soul shall become one with my weapon."

She cowered back, anger and fear marking her beautiful face. Grim threw the spear at her chest. Her tentacles went up to block it, but it went through all ten of them and straight to her heart.

With one last shrieking cry as she fell backward under the water. The water turned black, the color of her body fluids. It was as if she was rotten. The spear appeared from the water and came back to its owner. A black cloud followed behind the spear. "Death is only the beginning of your suffering." He spoke to the black cloud hovering in front of him. The spear became his scythe again and the cloud was sucked into the scythe before disappearing.

"What did you do?" I stood behind him.

"I saved countless lives by taking one. She will suffer eternally now." Something glowed in the black water, soon the water was clear again. Grim dove into the lake. I held my own breath until his head appeared above water. He strode out of the water, slipping something white and shiny into his dark jeans. He moved toward me, grabbed my waist, and tossed me over his shoulder.

"Now, what are you doing?" I jerked around on his shoulder. We entered that certain darkness again—then light, I knew he was using his power to take us somewhere else. He dropped me on my butt when we arrived at the new destination. We were at a hospital. It was crowded, nurses and doctors ran around frantically. I blinked my eyes, adjusting them to the bright florescent lights. Machine noises, doctors yelling, and the steady 'beep' of someone's lifeline filled my ears. I pinched my noise, I was never able to handle the smell of a hospital. It smelt of death, disease, and cleaning supplies.

I watched as people walked by, never even looking at us. It was as if we weren't there. "They can't see us?" He nodded. "What are we doing here?"

I followed through the halls. He looked back at me once. "I showed you the bad. Now I will show you the good." I frowned, confused. I couldn't see anything in the hospital being good. He stopped at room 303. I watched him go through it. I looked around and studied the door. Could I do that too? No one could see me. I decided to test it with my hand first. I gasped when my hand went straight through the door. *So, this was what it was like for ghosts*. I slipped into the room.

My smile dropped when I entered the room. It was easy to see what was happening. Several family members stood next to an elderly man lying in the hospital bed. A middle-aged man and two women. The women were crying. The doctor stood on the other side across from them. They all waited as the old man's breaths grew further apart and more faint. He was dying.

That was when I noticed someone else in the room. She too was old. She stood next to the doctor, tears were in her eyes as she gazed down at the man. They were happy tears yet sad. She was already dead.

Grim moved until he was next to her. She didn't even mind that he was standing next to her. The doctor stepped away to the give the family privacy. One of the women grabbed the old man's hand and smiled, despite the tears falling down her cheeks. "You will be with Mom soon. I'm sure she's waiting for you." I stood amazed when I realized who the old lady was. She was his wife. I watched as she smiled at her children.

The monitor bottomed out, the man's heart stopped beating. It didn't matter how much time you had to prepare yourself, the moment you lost a loved one, your heart literally breaks. My chest tightened, remembering the moment I lost Dad the same way. The room was quiet before the sobs broke out in the room. I felt emotional—sad for these people that I didn't even know. The old man rose from his body as a ghost. He saw his children first and his eyes filled with tears. His wife gently touched her ghostly hand over his, that's when he looked at her. He wore the biggest smile. A tear escaped my eye at their reunion. It was so easy to see how strong their love for one another was. He moved away from his corpse so that he could stand beside her. They embraced each other with a hug and kiss. Then they turned to Grim and nodded to him.

It made me wonder just how long the old lady waited for her husband so they could leave this world together. They gave a silent farewell to their grieving children although they couldn't see. Their goodbyes were over. Grim's scythe materialized in his hand. He pointed it and a bright circular path formed beside them. So bright that I couldn't look at it directly. I squinted my eyes trying to focus on the couple. They walked hand and hand in it together.

The path closed. I stood amazed. I just saw the gateway to Heaven. Grim walked to me. He reached for my hand and I already knew he was going to take us somewhere else. The darkness always came before the light and we were standing in the middle of the road in front of Deb's. The sky boomed with thunder. It was raining and coming down hard. We were already soaked, and by we, I meant Killian and me. He had changed back. Our hands were still entwined. I smiled, still feeling the emotions from everything I just witnessed. I pushed my hair out of my face with my free hand, not wanting to let go of his. He used his hand to help me move it behind my ear, not letting go of my hand either. "I didn't know death could be so..."

"Beautiful." His eyes met mine. The rain rolled off his cheeks, dripping from his chin. His dark hair clung over his forehead, hiding part of his eyes. I wanted to move it out of his eyes... His hand tightened over mine and the other lazily touched my cheek. "So beautiful." I could barely hear him over the rain. Rain dripped in my eyes and I had to blink. I had to let go of his hand to wipe my eyes.

"Why are we standing in the rain?" I asked. Thunder boomed causing me to jump against him. I grabbed his leather jacket. Then everything that happened next spun me out of my own control. His hand gripped my waist, pulling me in when I could already get no closer. I sucked in air as his face loomed over mine. The features of his face matched the storm. Wild and always unexpected. He pressed my chin up with force from his thumb. His mouth crushed over top mine. I could only sigh into his mouth because nothing felt so perfect. His hand left my cheek and tangled itself in my hair. My hands found his shirt. I gripped his sides, melting into him.

This wasn't kissing, his mouth continued to devour mine. He pushed onward, my inexperience didn't slow him. His hand found my chin again and forced me to open to him more. Our tongues collided and my heart hammered. I felt my mind slipping. Heat pooled through every part of my body like nothing I felt before. It felt amazing. It felt dangerous. I loved it.

The door to Deb's opened and a group of teenagers ran out in the rain, laughing, hurrying to their cars. His kiss slowed until his lips hovered near mine. Not touching, but not wanting to part either. I felt his breath fan my cheek. Which caused an ache that I'd never felt before spread in the pit of my stomach. It was a dark pleasure that threatened to shatter me to the core. He kissed my nose before leaning away, putting some distance between us. I could finally breathe, but the loss I felt made me wish he never stopped. His lips were swollen and red, the tip of his nose was also. The kiss still imprinted itself on him causing me to smile. He smiled back at me, lazy and sweet, exposing himself to me even more. Thunder crackled.

"You are dangerous, Melanie Rose," he whispered. I shook my head and laughed. I never knew what actual happiness felt like until that moment.

We parted after he walked me to the car. He disappeared in the rain once I was safely in my car. I stared at the rain, smiling but also disappointed that he left me. I noticed the light blinking on my cell phone when I started the car. I was freezing and soaking wet. I hoped I didn't get sick. I grabbed my phone from the passenger seat. Twenty-three missed calls. All of them were from Ryan. I sighed, dropping the phone back on the seat and drove home.

I went to my room once I was home before Mom took notice that I was drenched. I forgot to stop at the library. It was already closed by the time I got back with Killian. I grabbed some clothes and went to take a long hot bath. I turned the radio down low. I grinned to myself as I swayed my hands around in the soapy water. I thought of the kiss and touched my lips. I giggled and realized how silly I was acting and stopped. What in the world is wrong with me? I slid my head under the water and came back up.

When I thought of Ryan, I felt guilty. We were only friends. That didn't matter, I knew his feelings and I thought mine were once the same. Things were changing—things were getting complicated. I wasn't sure how I felt. I moved my legs around in the water. What did that kiss mean?

I let the water out of the tub and stepped out. My mood was ruined with doubts and worries. I thought pushing Ryan would keep him safe. I only hurt him and I justified that by telling myself he would be safe. I've always knew my feelings for Ryan, then why....

Why did I kiss Killian? *Grim Reaper took my first kiss.*

I dried myself off and put on my pajamas. When I entered my room, my stomach did this crazy flop when I saw Killian laying across the foot of my bed. He opened his eyes when he heard the door shut. "You're in my room."

"Yeah." He rose. He whistled as he glanced around the room like he never been here before. "Nice and cozy." he added. I rubbed my neck and Killian eyed the spot I rubbed. He was acting different and I wasn't sure at all how I was supposed to act. He let out a sigh. "What's wrong? Is there any particular reason why you're suddenly so shy?" he asked, arching his brow. He moved his hand to his side and gave me a devilish smile. "I think I might have the imprints of your fingernails on my side." I blushed, remembering the way I had been clinging to him while we kissed.

"Will you stop?" I glared, wanting to hide my embarrassment. I was so nervous.

"Stop what?"

"Stop teasing me. You're the one that kissed me."

"Relax. We won't do it again." He surrendered his hands in the air to make his point. I was disappointed that he said it so easily. "Unless, that's what you want then by all means, kiss the Underworld out of me." Something dangerous flickered in his eyes. A dark promise. The spiraling heat that I felt in the pit of my stomach came raging back at his words. I swallowed hard, looking away.

"I'm going to sleep," I said quickly, hurrying to my bed and hiding under the covers. My foot touched his side where he sat at the edge of the bed. I let it linger close to him. I closed my eyes and tried to think about sleeping.

He moved. He felt closer. *Sleep. Sleep. Sleep.* I held the cover over my face, squinting my eyes shut. He left the bed. I heard his boots glide across the floor. What was he doing? He went quiet several seconds before he moved again. I jumped up and sighed. "I can't sleep with you making noise."

He paced the room, raking his hand through his hair. He looked a little more out of control than usual. He stopped and glared at me. I moved my legs under the cover trying to get comfortable. He eyed the movement. "Will you stop moving around so much? You're the one making all the noise." I looked at him funny.

"You're the one stalking around my room like a panther," I growled back.

"You're killing me," he grumbled, giving me a pitiful smile.

"I'm not doing anything."

My door opened. "Why are you yelling?"
Mom stood in the doorway. I looked to where
Killian was. He already disappeared. I sighed.

"I thought I seen a bug," I grumbled. "A very
big bug."

CHAPTER TWELVE

I moaned as his fingers brushed over my belly. His body laid between my legs as he planted kisses on my stomach. When I tried to wiggle free, he tightened his grip on my hip. His fingers traced over my waist, traveling down to my thighs. Pleasure I'd never known caused goosebumps to breakout all over me.

"You're so sensitive, I'm barely touching you." He gazed up at me, mouth hovering above my navel. Then he continued with his kisses, intoxicating my senses until his mouth found my panties. There was a lustful look in his eyes as he admired them. "You're so beautiful," he whispered, his breath heating my panties. He was too much for me. I moved beneath his hold. His

247

words were too much. His touch was setting me on fire. I wanted to escape this beautiful agony. But the thought of breaking free of the pleasure his touch promised... I couldn't. I could only whimper in reply.

He pressed his face into my core, I arched my back just as his tongue swiped over my panties. I cried out. His hands held down my hips and his finger twirled under the string before yanking them off. He wasn't gentle, he was rough. My legs were lifted in the air so that he could slide the panties off. He tossed them in the floor. When I tried to place my legs back down, he held them up. He traced them with his eyes, sliding his hand down until he found my butt cheek. He cupped one side of it before smacking it. I whimpered, not use to the sting. The feeling also caused a reaction between my thighs. I felt the trickle of something wet escape my sex.

He spread my legs apart. His eyes devoured my nakedness. He moved his hand between my thigh, I found myself lifting my butt off the bed to meet his touch. Once he did, I felt as if I dissolved into a puddle at his feet. "You're so wet." My cheeks flushed but not from embarrassment, I was too far gone for that. I lifted my hips, pressing myself into his hand, needing and wanting everything he offered.

He dropped my legs down and bent over my stomach, trailing kisses down until he was between my thighs. When his mouth came down over that part of me, I went wild for him. It felt amazing. I grabbed his hair, raking my nails over his scalp. His finger slipped inside my most intimate place and I exploded in a million pieces.

"Killian," my voice laced with pleasure.

"It's not over, Love." He leaned over me. I reached out and touched his chest, something I couldn't do when he was between my legs. He was sexy. And powerful. My body almost came undone again at the mere sight of him. "You're mine," he growled. I closed my eyes and moaned.

"You're mine," he spoke again, but his voice was somehow different. I opened my eyes and saw the horror. Grim lay above me, in Killian's place. One of his boned fingers raked against my naked chest before pinching my nipple.

I screamed, eyes opening. I found myself floating in the air above my bed. Everything in the room was floating. Killian's hands made contact with my waist and everything fell to the ground, including me, I fell on my bed. He moved on the bed next to me. I looked around at the mess in my room. But worst of all, Mom might have heard. The thought of her witnessing something like that again made me sick.

I finally noticed the glow on my skin. "That's not possible." Killian spoke, looking both shocked and worried.

"What's happening?" I gawked at my arms. I feared what was happening to me. The glow underneath my skin seemed to dim until it completely faded away.

"The Vessel." He stared at my arm as he spoke. "It's like it's been awakened."

"That just now." I looked around the room before adding, "That was the Vessel? The power that's inside me?" I whispered.

He nodded before a frown appeared on his handsome face. "This shouldn't be possible. It doesn't make sense." He shook his head. He brought his hand up to touch my cheek. I flinched when I remembered the dream I had. My cheeks heated. Jeez, one kiss from him and I'm already fantasizing about him. "Are you okay?" He looked worried.

"Yeah." I spoke too soon. The mark on my chest burned my skin and I winced. Killian quickly tugged at my shirt, exposing the X. It glowed crimson red.

He cursed and met my eyes. "He knows."

———

Killian told me it was best not to go to

school. I called Mom while she was at work and faked a cough. She believed me. No, she never thought not to believe me. I realized I was lying a lot to her lately. Not something I ever did besides hiding the fact that I saw ghosts.

I stepped in front of the mirror in my room and knew the girl I was looking at was completely different than two weeks ago. It was sad yet funny how almost getting killed repeatedly, meeting Grim Reaper, and finding out that my life was this way because a demon was after me, changed a person. The Melanie from two weeks ago was timid and afraid, not sure of anything. Or why her life was this way. She lived in constant fear every day and never knew why. And how ironic that the thing that wanted her went by the name Fear? But I wasn't her anymore.

Now, I was sick and tired. Sick of this never-ending fear of the future. And so tired of being controlled by it. I wasn't completely clueless now. Which made things easier to accept. I finally felt like I could understand. I saw ghosts because of the contact Fear made with me when I was a child. Fear wanted me because I carried a power within me. One that I never knew about until now. And it had started to awaken inside of me. A normal human girl. That shouldn't have been possible—according to Killian. Not until my death should it had been activated.

But it did.

Then came the scarier part. More demons will come for me eventually when they find out of my existence. The Vessel was putting my life at stake. A power I still knew nothing about. It put everyone I loved in danger. Ghosts disappeared around me because Grim was close by but in return, demons were taking place. Something much worse.

But I did have Killian. My protector.

I gazed into the mirror and noticed him behind me. He met my eyes in the mirror. His shoulders were tense; I could feel the uneasy energy in the room coming from him. I simply looked at him. I had no idea where he fit into everything. I thought he hated me when we first met. Which I felt the same way... Now, his anger scared me. What was his anger directed toward? Did I dare to think that his anger was worry for my safety? Did he, perhaps... care what happened to me? Or was it because it was his job? I turned around to face him slowly. "How is staying home from school going to do me any good?"

I trusted him now. Even when he was scary, deep down I knew I could count on him. I just hoped those feelings were to be trusted. His face was conflicted with so many emotions, as if he was thinking of all his problems one after another. He sighed. "He's gotten out of control over the centuries. This should have never happened."

I studied him. "You say that a lot."

"What?" He looked up."

"*This should have never happened. This shouldn't be possible.*" I answered, placing my hand on my hip. "But it has. And who is he?" I dropped my hands to my sides, the fear clawing at my chest that I fought to ignore. "Do you mean Fear? That is what you called him, I believe."

"Yeah. Before I was Grim, I was," he hesitated, not sure he wanted to continue. "He was a friend, or at least I thought so. He wasn't like this before..."

A shiver ran up my spine. "How can someone be friends with something so evil?" He held up his hands when he seen the hostile look in my eyes.

"No, I didn't explain that right. Fear's an entity as well. I was friends with the demon he merged with. Not the entity himself. It was a long time ago, but my guess is that it's the reason I was sent here to keep you safe."

I remembered back to the day Fear attacked me in the classroom. I could remember the way I felt in his presence. It was like standing in front of pure evil. I couldn't see Killian ever being friends with something so evil. Killian wasn't at all human like me, but I knew he wasn't evil. Really scary, yes. A lot dangerous, oh yeah! He was amazingly powerful and I was beginning to wonder if there was anything he couldn't do. When I first met him, I thought he was bad. But I knew better now. He was nothing like Fear.

"I never saw what attacked me that day," I whispered, my mind going back to that dark time. Where my life went from happy and bright to dark and terrifying. "But what I felt," I shook my head, clenching my hands together, "was a monster. It felt evil and wrong. It was as if everything deceitful and bad in this world was covered in flesh in that room with me. I can never forget that feeling."

"When he merged with Fear, he took all his traits. He became the monster himself."

"Are you somehow trying to defend him?" I accused.

He shook his head, replying immediately.

"Never. I'm only saying the demon he was before the merge isn't the monster he is today."

I took three steps, moving closer to him. "You keep saying merge, what do you mean?"

"It's something that happens between a demon and entity. When a demon reaches a maturing age, an entity can choose a demon to merge with."

"I don't get it."

He sighed. "It's a bond. The demon chooses to share his body and mind with the entity. They become one being. For eternity."

I wrinkled my nose. "So, something like lovers?"

He groaned, slapping his hand over his face. "You wouldn't understand. You're just a—"

"No, go on," I placed my index finger on my lips to let him know that I would shut up. "I'm really curious," I added quietly.

He smiled. "Demons are not very powerful on their own. Most are low ranking demons with little or no power. You've seen the wolf demons, other than brute strength alone and a big bite, they have no special powers." I nodded and he arched his eyebrow. "Take incubus and succubus demons." I opened my mouth to say something and his hand went over my mouth. I wanted to ask what those demons were. I frowned. "They are sex demons. In order to survive, they feed off of their sexual appetites." He grinned and studied my reaction as if he only spoke of those sort of demons to tease me. I blushed and looked away. "Besides, the art of seduction and power of persuasion, they have no power." He waited for another reaction. I gave him none.

"My point," he grabbed his chin. "So many demons are like that. Demons love power. They hate to feel weak. That is why so many try to merge with an entity."

"It happens a lot?" I wondered.

He nodded. "Afraid so. They are many merges. Marcus merged with Fear the same day I did with Grim." I was stunned for a moment, trying to understand what that meant. Then it all made sense. My mouth formed an O when I understood. He grinned.

"So, that explains the way you change into him the way you do." He nodded again. It was strange yet so fascinating. "What kind of demon was/are you?" I asked.

He moved quickly, taking my hand and lifting it in the air above my head. He kept pressing my hand further up until I had to stand on my tiptoes. He moved my hand in the air in his direction causing me to tiptoe closer until my breasts were brushing against his chest. His grin turned cocky as his other hand moved behind me and pressed against the bottom of my back. My breath got lost somewhere in between as he pushed my hips into his. His finger slipped underneath my shirt and grazed my back. A new sensation rippled through my stomach in the direction of my thighs. His smell invaded my senses, dark and manly. It smelled sinful and naughty, making me think of chocolate and coffee. It was like I could taste the exotic smell of him with my mind. I completely lost myself in his embrace.

He stole my lips with only a peck. A brief contact that ended too soon and released my hand that he held in the air. I crumbled to the floor at his feet, unable to catch myself. My heart thudded, ears burned, my whole body was on fire, and felt the ache of his missing touch. I stared at the carpet. I couldn't look up knowing his smile would be pure mischief.

I wished on everything fierce for him to kiss me again. The craving grew inside of me for him, for everything he was. Everything he made me feel. But because of that, I stood up. I cooled my features, tampering down the need I felt for him. It wasn't the right time when I still wasn't sure what he was to me. He was becoming something to me, though... That both terrified and excited me.

I hardened my features before I looked up to

meet his smug face. His lips were tilted in to a half smile, smoldering look. "So, you're one of the sex demons?" I asked.

"Incubus." He nodded, pleased with himself.

"You could have just said that." I was embarrassed, but I couldn't stop looking at his lips. "You and your guessing games," I muttered.

"Why would I tell you and miss the opportunity to kiss you again?" he teased, grabbing a strand of my hair laying over my collarbone.

"That wasn't a kiss," I squeaked and quickly looked down after saying it.

I looked up to see his teeth flash with his perfect smile. "Oh?"

"Barely a peck," I muttered.

"Shall we do it again?"

The house door opened downstairs and a second later I heard it click back shut. Mom was home from work. "Melanie, how are you feeling?" Mom called out, I heard her shoes climbing the stairs. Killian sighed, disappointment clear on his face.

"Your mom has great timing; rain check?" His eyes twinkled with his smile. I knew he probably meant kissing. I hid my blush and he disappeared as Mom opened the door. I was getting use to his disappearing acts.

She smiled as she peeked in the door. "It's just my stomach, but it's killing me. I'm just gonna lie back down." I walked to my bed and laid down, placing the covers over me.

"Yeah, probably best." She nodded. "Do you want me to make you anything?"

I shook my head. "No, thanks."

"Okay. I'm going to shower and head to the store before I lie down to get a couple hours of rest before work tonight." I nodded as she closed my door.

I waited until I heard her leave before climbing back out of bed. I messed around by my bookshelf waiting on Killian to reappear. He couldn't have gone anywhere far. Especially when it was becoming more dangerous for me to be alone. My cell phone rang on the nightstand, I picked it up. Ryan. I studied the phone, struggling with whether I should answer or not. I couldn't keep ignoring him. I slid the answer button across the phone and brought it to my ear. "Melanie." His relieved voice drifted through the phone before I could even answer. It felt good to hear his voice. The thought of staying away from him bothered me even when I knew it was for the best.

"Hey."

"I'm sorry," he said immediately. I was the one who should be apologizing. "I got worried when I didn't see you at school."

"Killian didn't think it was a good idea for me to go to school today. He's thinks something bad is about to happen."

He went quiet before going off in my ear. "I don't trust him or any of this! I should be with you."

"Ryan, no," I quickly replied. "I'm okay.

Please, stay out of it. It's too dangerous." He swore over the phone before letting out a long sigh.

"I gotta go, second period already started." He hung up before I could tell him goodbye.

"Foolish human. How does he think to protect you when he is a human himself?" I hadn't realized Killian was in the room. I looked behind me and saw him standing next to the window, an unpleasant scowl plastered on his hardened features. I knew it was because of Ryan. He had that effect on him.

"He cares about me." I defended Ryan. As old as Killian claimed to be, he didn't seem very familiar with relationships. Friend or otherwise, people cared for one another. It made the world continue on despite the evil in the world. I guess demons weren't the same.

"You should tell him how you feel. He's going nuts because of you. He might back off if he knows your feelings." he growled, turning away from me and placing his hand against the wall as he looked outside. I simply looked at his back unsure that he said that. What was he thinking? Did he honestly tell me that? He was always unreadable except for his anger that he always showed in leaps and bounds. Did nothing phase him? Did he not care about what I felt for Ryan?

I wished I knew what was going on in that head of his. I thought that we were finally making some sort of connection. I thought he might have felt something toward me. I was probably wrong. No, I misread his kiss for something more because it might have been something earth shattering for me; it meant nothing to him. Where were my thoughts even going?

I was too far upset now to think about it, though. "Are you saying I should be with Ryan?" My voice dripped with anger.

He turned back around, his eyes turning liquid black as he stalked toward me like I was his prey. I shivered with anticipation despite being mad. "Are you telling me you still want to be with him?" He slowly let the words out. I studied him, knowing my mistake and recognized his jealousy when it was boiling over in front of me. His words had confused me when meant the opposite of what he said. I had mistaken his anger for the wrong thing. He wanted to know my true feelings. As he drew closer, I moved back, falling atop the bed, nervous from what he planned to do. Once he was hovering over me, he grabbed me underneath my armpits and hauled me back to my feet. I eyed him warily as he glared down at me. The height difference was intimidating. "I think you are mistaking something, Melanie."

My heart flopped out of my chest when he said my name. A ripple of pleasure ran up my back. He really was jealous. I didn't know much about romance, but I recognized jealousy so easily. I had seen it enough in Tess's relationships. I tried not to think about how Ryan's jealousy had only annoyed me, but with Killian it was a happy feeling. Feminine power grew inside me, giving me enough courage to meet his deadly gaze. "What do you mean?" I replied haughtily.

"You should tell him how you really feel, not what he wants to hear you say. The truth."

I was finally the one to wear the cocky grin as I arched an eyebrow up at him. "Oh? Maybe I should tell him then." His eyes devoured me whole when I didn't give him the answer he was waiting for. I wouldn't admit my attraction to him. Nor would I admit my lingering feelings for Ryan. His nostrils flared, eyes going black again before his face began to relax and an appreciative smile came over him as he peered down at me.

"By all means," he agreed. His hand found my hair; tangling his fingers around my blonde strands. He lowered his head until we were eye level. I melted under his demanding gaze. How was I ever supposed to know how he felt when I was always turning into putty around him?

He broke our eye contact. His eyes darted to the door, his body stiffened, shoulders tensed and alarmed as if he was waiting for something to happen. I tilted my head to look at the door, but he was running through the door as I did. He didn't even bother opening it, he just slipped straight through it like a ghost. I followed him, opening the door because I couldn't do things the weird way like Killian. He wasn't upstairs. I heard a crashing sound downstairs, like things being tore apart. I didn't have time to worry about what Mom would do if she found out whatever they were destroying. I hurried downstairs and came face to face with Molly once I reached the bottom. Killian had a demon—or could be a ghost—pinned down against the broken coffee table. Well, I knew where the sound came from. The demon/whatever smiled up at Killian as if he didn't care he was about to die. That caused Killian to snarl.

I warily watched Molly, waiting on her to make her move. The little girl smiled bright, but it was an unpleasant one that made my skin crawl. "You're quite a nuisance," she sneered.

"You could just stop trying to kill me," I offered.

Her face lit up, she tilted her head back and laughed. "There is no need for that now the Vessel has awoken." I gulped. Killian had been right. Fear already knew.

"A lot of trouble to go through over this Vessel everyone speaks of. Are you sure it's worth it?" I muttered. The man Killian held down slowly began to fade away after Killian crushed his neck. He got up from his knees, shooting daggers with his eyes at Molly as he strode toward her. She sensed his movement coming from behind and jumped to the second floor. She turned around quickly, meeting my eyes.

"Dunno, Fear is the one that wants it, not me." She shrugged her shoulders as if she were tired of this conversation. "Nonetheless, I just do his bidding," she replied sharply, I got the sense she didn't care so much about the demon she worked for. "Which is why I am here. I came to deliver a message." Killian moved in front of me, his hand shot out in front of me in a protective manner as he watched Molly. He pushed me behind him further.

"He won't lay a hand on her. Tell him it's time to stop. I won't let him take her. *Ever.*" Killian sounded frightening even to me and his anger wasn't even directed toward me.

If Molly was afraid, she hid it well. She started down the stairs slowly, taking her time. She looked to him then to me. Her eyes caught more than I realized, her eyes darted to the way I clung to his back, gripping his leather jacket and the way he safely tucked me behind him. Her eyes lifted in amusement. "How interesting," she stated. Killian growled. "But that should be enough time for the job to be finished."

My eyes grew wide, unease filled my entire body. "What do you mean?" I yelled.

"Don't you get it?" She smiled. "You were not the target. I came to deliver a message. The message is a warning. It's what will continue to happen if you keep refusing to come to Fear. He doesn't like to wait. Even more so..." She glanced at Killian. "He doesn't like who is keeping you from him."

She tilted her head in mockery, placing a finger on her chin as if she were waiting. Killian grew tired of her games and grabbed her tiny body, swinging her into the wall causing pictures to fall and shatter once they hit the ground. "Enough games," he drew in a breath, probably to keep himself calm.

Molly hissed at him. She looked to me as he held her pinned against the wall by her shoulders. "He told me to tell you... 'Come to me' or," she laughed. "Whoops, I forgot." She was stalling, playing games and my worry grew. Killian roared, but she disappeared under his hold.

"What do you think she meant?" I whispered a few minutes after she disappeared. I feared something horrible and looked to Killian for an answer. He swore, ruffling his hair with his hand.

"She was distracting us, I'm not sure why." He prowled around the room, pacing and agitated. Somewhere in the process he began to fix the mess he had made, flicking his wrist around as if it were nothing.

"Mom just left for the store..." My stomach bottomed out at the thought of something happening to her. He stopped in his tracks, disappearing a moment later.

Time seemed to still in his absence as I waited for him to come back. I grabbed the phone off the kitchen counter and dialed Mom's cell. She picked up on the third ring. "Hello?"

I sighed in relief. "Mom."

"What's wrong?" I recognized her worried mother voice and knew I had caused her alarm.

"Nothing—" My cell phone was going off in my room upstairs. I hurried upstairs to answer it. "Let me call you back." I hung up and grabbed my cell phone. It was Tess.

"Hey, can I call you," I cut myself off when I heard her sobbing over the phone. Awful, horrid crying that flared my panic back to life. My heart thudded with sickening fear. "What's wrong?"

"Melanie." She hiccupped while she cried, hardly able to talk. "It's R-R-Ryan. He just wrecked his truck." My whole body went numb.

"What are you talking about? Tess? He was at school, I just got off the phone with him not too long ago." My voice came out weak and frantic, not wanting to believe what I was hearing.

She cried harder. "He left school. Something about going to check on you." I grabbed my mouth, bile rising in my throat. I fell to my knees as the tears streaked my face.

Molly's voice rung in my ear over and over. *I came to give you a warning.*

CHAPTER THIRTEEN

It was a nightmare. A horrible, horrible nightmare that I couldn't wake up from. I drove myself to Denver's hospital, not sure how I managed to when my mind was focused on Ryan. I found Tess in the waiting room. She was a mess, eyeliner smeared underneath her eyes and she started crying again when I arrived. It caused my own tears to start back as we ran to hug one another, needing that comfort from each other. She briefly told me what was going on. Apparently, they took Ryan to surgery the moment he arrived in the ambulance.

I called Mom during the time we were waiting and told her what happened. This happened to be her workplace, she rushed over right after I called. I placed my head on my knees and watched Tess pace the floor as we waited to hear from the doctor. Mom offered to grab us a bite to eat in the cafeteria but the thought of food made my nervous stomach queasy.

It wasn't until two hours, maybe longer, before Linda, Ryan's mom, rushed in carrying her overpriced handbag and was typing furiously on her cell phone. When she finally looked up to see her daughter, she plastered a worried expression on her face. I never felt so annoyed with their parents until this moment. Even when they weren't around, I thought they still cared for them, but why did it never seem that way to me. Was it because my own parents were so different. Ryan and Tess always had the best clothes, latest phones, and nicest cars. Their parents made sure of that, but lack of warmth and love from their parents were always visible to me.

I watched as Linda kissed Tess's cheek and wrapped her into a hug. Tess's expression was unreadable as her mom hugged her. "Where's Dad?" she asked Linda as she broke away from the hug.

She sighed, leading them to some chairs to sit down. "He's in Kansas working. He's not going to be able to make it today." Tess glared at her mother.

"His only son is in surgery from a wreck!" Tess accused.

"It's not that simple."

Tess didn't reply and the waiting room grew intensely quiet. Linda finally noticed us sitting on the other side of the room. "Oh, I didn't see you guys." She smiled, trying to hide her startled look. I simply nodded, unable to muster anything nice to say.

"Yes, we care a lot about Ryan." I didn't miss the icy tone in Mom's voice as she glared at Linda. Mom's protective instincts were showing, she thought of my friends as one of her own. She spent many nights feeding us all.

The room descended into quietness again until another family joined us waiting for someone to get out of surgery. Mom left to pick Alex up from school, bringing him back to the hospital with her. Finally, after what felt like a lifetime, a doctor walked out looking exhausted. "Ryan Jones's family?" His accent was thick, but understandable and we all rushed toward him.

"I'm his mother. How is my son?" Linda plastered a worried look on her face.

The doctor sighed, clicking the pen in his hand before putting it in his coat pocket. "He's stable for now." My head spun. What did that mean?

"What happened? What's wrong with him?" Tess asked, sounding just as helpless as we all felt.

"He suffered some head trauma. On top of that, he broke several ribs puncturing his lung. We found some internal bleeding that we managed to stop. Both legs are broken. That is why the surgery took so long. We have him sedated. I will tell you now just so that you don't worry when you see it. We are going to keep him on a ventilator for tonight as a precaution." I heard what he was saying, but my mind and heart did not know how to process it. I staggered backward and Alex was there to grab my hand. I felt numb.

Tess started crying and my mom hugged her. Linda covered her mouth with her hand, fear and sincerity reflecting through her eyes. It was real fear this time. "We've put him in ICU. Intensive care unit. You guys can visit him during the visiting hours." He nodded before walking away.

The walk to get to ICU felt like it took a lifetime. We had to press a button outside of the door that paged the nurses. Thankfully, it was visiting hours but only two could see him at a time. I frowned as I watched Tess and Linda go through the doors to see him. I paced the door waiting for one of them to come out.

Mom gently grabbed my shoulder as if to comfort me. Alex looked small standing against the hallway wall. His head was lowered, nervous. I wanted to be there for him, but I didn't even know how to handle it myself.

My guilty conscious was eating me alive.

The door opened and Linda stepped out dabbing her eyes with a tissue. Her makeup was ruined from the tears she spilled. Her lip did a small tremble as she met my eyes. If she was this way, it only showed just how bad the situation was. When she tried to speak, it came out as a cry. "You go see him. I can't see him like that." With those words, she hurried down the hall.

Mom squeezed my shoulder. "He will be okay." I barely nodded, praying she was right. I went in. Some of the ICU rooms beds were exposed and I saw patients as I walked by. Other rooms were private, I recognized the person sobbing as I grew closer to Ryan's room. This unit was especially quiet; everyone spoke in hushed conversations and all I could hear was the steady beeping of machines. I found his room. I saw him on the bed as I walked in and I crumbled to the floor. I cried and grabbed the foot of the hospital bed for support. Tess lay over his chest, but not actually putting any weight on him. He was unrecognizable, his body and face looked as it were swollen from all the bruises. Some type of metal rods stuck out of his legs that went into his bones. He wore a hospital gown, but he hadn't been cleaned up since the wreck. Blood covered his handsome face and parts of his arms. Tess quickly hid his legs underneath the small sheet as if to hide it from our view. He had a nasty gash above his left eye. But the most frightening thing was the tube that went into his mouth and the way his chest rose and fell with the machine.

Still crying, I stood up and managed to move next to Tess where she stood. The look she gave me caused my heart to clench knowing we felt the same pain. I found his hand and wrapped my fingers into his, giving it a gentle squeeze before leaning over and whispering in his ear. "I'm so sorry." My tear fell and hit his cheek.

———————

Tess and I stayed at the hospital that night. I missed school again the next day, but Mom never said a word. Alex stayed with Mom's sister—our aunt Brenda—while she had to work. Her little boy was almost the same age as Alex and they go to school together. Mom constantly checked on us throughout the night when she got the chance. We slept in the waiting room, Linda was back early the next morning. I found myself walking the halls alone as I let Tess talk with her mom.

I went to the cafeteria and bought a coffee. I only drunk coffee when I was tired, I hated it, but I needed something. I took a sip. It was horrible. I drank it anyway. The cafeteria was empty besides a couple a few tables away from me and the cooks.

Someone moved next to me and took a seat. I didn't have to lift my head from the table to know who it was. I always knew his presence, it filled up the entire room every time I was close to him. I peeked out from my arm to see him staring at me. His face reflected sadness and concern for me or Ryan, I did not know.

I sniffled, wanting to cry again just because he was here. I lifted my face and pinched my nose hoping that would prevent me from doing so. He scooted his chair closer and pulled me back until I was entrapped in his embrace. I somehow maneuvered myself in his strong hug so that I could wrap my hands around him, pressing my ear against his chest. I could hear the steady rhythm of his heartbeat. My worries seemed to evaporate in his presence, inside his arms.

This was all my fault. The horrible part was that no one knew except me. Ryan didn't deserve what happened to him. All he ever did was care for me. I felt so much hatred for myself. I didn't even know if he would be okay. But why was I hugging Killian when the person that's been there for me half my life is laying in the hospital bed. Better yet, the Grim Reaper, someone I barely knew. I jumped up so abruptly, the chair squeaked as it slid across the floor. Killian looked up to me surprised.

I hurried away. I felt him following after me. *Don't follow me. Don't.* "Melanie." I ignored the strange pull that always drew me to him. The one that seemed to tug at my heart and mind. I opened the cafeteria door and stepped into the halls. I heard his deep sigh, one of impatience as he snagged my arm from behind and pulled me around to face him.

I tried to keep my expression neutral. "What is it?" I asked.

"Whatever you're thinking. Whatever you're feeling. Don't. He's going to be okay." I jerked my arm away from him.

"This is my fault." I gripped my palms. "Because things are happening to me that shouldn't be. Things that shouldn't even be real are after me."

He glanced back and forth in the hallway. "I

don't think this is the best place for this conversation."

"I can't do this anymore."

His forehead wrinkled, not quite sure what I meant. "What do you mean?"

"I didn't ask for this. Why is it happening to me? I just want to be normal. No." I shook my head. "I wished things where back to the way they were before I met you. When seeing ghosts was my only problem. Not dealing with demons. Or you."

He flinched at my words, something flickered in his eyes. Was it sadness? Or did I hurt him? My throat twisted, I hadn't meant to say that the way it had come out, but I couldn't go back on what I said. Because a part of me felt that way. "You don't actually mean that," he whispered. I thought he was going to reach out to me, but he changed his mind.

I couldn't see anything, the tears in my eyes that I refused to blink out blurred my vision. I finally reached up and wiped my eyes. "I can't lose him. He's all I ever really had." My voice was soft from the crying, but it never wavered. I was telling the truth. I loved Ryan. I didn't know what that love was anymore, but it was special.

His face hardened, I saw him slowly slipping back on his mask, tucking away every emotion he felt inside. I knew how my words sounded. I pretty much told him I couldn't lose Ryan, but I could lose him. He took a step back. I felt feverish, my heart beat frantically, my whole body convulsed begging me to take back what I said. This feeling, my heart must know. What I was feeling was more than hurt.

It was a heartbreak.

A loss.

The loss of something so fragile and precious before I even got to know it.

CHAPTER FOURTEEN

"The police said he most likely lost control of his truck when his tire blew out. Not to mention he was in a curve when it happened causing the truck to flip into the ditch." Tess took a drink of her iced tea before pulling her phone from her back pocket. "Mom sent me pictures of the truck."

I took the phone from her hand and glanced at the image. There the truck was, flipped on its top next to the small cliff I passed going to school every morning. The roof of the truck was smashed completely in and a tire was missing. I swiped my finger over the screen to look at the next picture. They had the truck towed back to their house in this picture. Now that the truck was laying on its top, I could see the real damage. I gripped the phone, a violent shudder raking over my body. How could a person survive this accident? The top was completely smashed in almost; I could see where they bent what was left of the door to get Ryan out. The truck was destroyed. I handed the phone back to Tess unable to look any longer. "I want to speak to him. I wished they would let him wake up just so I know that he's going to be okay," Tess whimpered. She leaned into me and I her, using each other for support.

I felt the same as Tess. I understood why they chose to keep him sedated, but for a minute, just a minute, I'd like to see his big brown eyes and for him to tell me he was okay. Leaning against Tess, I looked upward, trying to contain my tears and realized this was it, that moment I realized my person must be Ryan. Always Ryan. This ache in my chest hurt so bad. Once he was awake, I'd tell him how I felt. How much he meant to me. I wouldn't hold back any more, holding back from him only drove him to be more reckless. I wouldn't hold back because of the danger; it was too late for that now. Killian's handsome face flashed through my mind and I shook my head, swallowing the lump in my throat. I wouldn't tell him about how much I was affected by the Grim Reaper that was sent to keep me safe. Or how the single thought of his name lit up my entire being. No, Ryan was too good for that. Too sweet. He deserved better.

I didn't know what to do now. I took a deep breath, getting a whiff of Tess's strawberry shampoo before stepping away from her. Waiting was hard. I couldn't do it. Besides, I couldn't wait. Who would be Fear's next target? Mike walked in as I was stepping out, Tess gave a small smile when she saw him. She buried her face in his chest when he reached out to her.

Now that Mike was there for Tess; I could relax. I had to do something. No one else needed to get hurt because of me. I was so sick of Fear taking everything from me. That one emotion has controlled my whole life since the day I met him in the classroom. Fear destroyed my life, marked my skin permanently with a sick reminder of him, leaving me haunted by ghosts. Because of that, I lived in fear, afraid to do anything worth doing with my life. My face was burning with so much hate, I gripped my pants to calm myself.

Funny how I thought fear was only an emotion. Now I knew it was a very real monster that trapped me with fear. It felt so foolish now, being afraid for so long. I wanted to stand up for myself, but I didn't know how to. Today, I wouldn't fear Fear. If he wanted me, I'd let him have me. I would learn to fight back.

Somehow.

I went to see Ryan in the ICU. He still had the ventilator. They said it was only a precaution, but worry seeped into my chest telling me otherwise. Was he not in the safe yet? What weren't they saying? Or what did his mom know...? I grabbed his hand, trying to find it in me to give him a smile as I moved a strand of matted hair off his forehead.

It didn't look like Ryan laying here so broken down and lifeless.

It was at that moment, I made another promise to myself. I would find a way to protect myself so that no one would get hurt because of me. I lowered my face to his and placed a small kiss on his jaw. His skin was cool to the touch, another reminder this wasn't the boy I've known for so long. Here, in this room, on this bed, he was a sleeping boy. Just a boy, fighting for his life. Did he get to think of his life while he was in this state? I closed my eyes, shaking the thoughts from my mind. "I can't let this happen to anyone else." I reopened my eyes and told him, hoping he could hear me. "I promise I will find a way to fight back. I'm trying not to be afraid anymore. So, please open your eyes, okay?" I whispered. The room was quiet, the steady rhythm of the machine helping Ryan breathe grew louder in my ears as I stared at him until I finally just left the room.

As I walked a couple rooms away, a monitor

started beeping out of control. Several nurses and doctors began rushing over to the room next to Ryan's. My whole body tingled as I froze in place, afraid to move as I listened. A male doctor yelled and nurses scrambled, rummaging and plastic being tore open as the machine continued to beat frantically. "We're losing him," a nurse yelled. I couldn't not look any longer, I whirled around to see the group working hard to keep the man alive on the bed. But I wished I hadn't turned around.

Grim materialized in the room, in front of the bed. Nurses went through him as they hurriedly moved around the bed. The man's heart rate began to plummet, causing everyone to try harder, but I knew it wouldn't be enough. It was already over for the man. Grim being in the room only proved it. The man was laying in his death bed. His heart rate bottomed out completely, the machines stopped, and the room fell silent. One of the nurses dropped her head as the doctor looked at his watched. "Time of death 2:13 P.M."

"Miss." I looked to see an older nurse next to me. "I'm gonna have to ask you to leave." I let her walk me to the ICU entrance as I turned to stare at Grim's back before leaving. He looked at me just as the nurse shut the door in my face.

I sighed, shaky and ashamed because a single thought drifted in my head as the man died.

Thank God it wasn't Ryan.

———

That evening, sometime after school had ended, the hospital was covered with people that we went to school with. They all wanted to visit, but none of them could. People brought Tess and Linda money and food for their hospital stay as well as prayers and comfort. I slipped away to catch my breath. I didn't do well with these people. I knew that someone would be out soon enough to send them all home as loud as they were being.

My mind drifted to Killian and when I would see him again as the voices grew fainter the further away I got from the others. And of course, in Killian fashion, and if he could tell when I was thinking of him, he appeared around the corner of the hallway. His dark clothing stood out underneath the bright fluorescent lights of the hospital. He placed his hands in each of his pants pockets before looking down at me. I say 'down' because he's just impossibly huge. I need to shorten him somehow, but there was no time to be thinking of all the things I noticed about him. "We need to talk," I said quickly.

He nodded. "Yeah. We do." His deep, rich voice caused a shiver to run up my spine the more I was around him. Only this time it was his cold, harshness in each word that caused me to shiver. "But not here." He reached his hand out to me and it caused me to think back to all the times he had done so before. He was always doing so out of protection and concern, always with the hint of worry and warrior mixed together. Other times, like the night that changed how much I felt about him, when he offered it then, I could see worry. I could see he wanted my acceptance, to know him. Most of all, he wanted my trust. Maybe, even that night, I probably even saw uncertainty flash in his eyes, not sure of himself or me, or what we were doing. It was a shy feeling for both of us. But this time, this was different....

His face was blank, completely devoid of any emotion. I couldn't tell what he was thinking. His icy glare pierced and poked at my heart and it hurt more than I wanted to admit. I sensed no emotion. Nothing. Just the harsh glare of his eyes as he stared down at me. I deserved this much, but it didn't mean I liked it. I took his hand. I merely blinked and we were suddenly on the roof of the hospital. I stared down at the ongoing traffic and busy parking lot. It was cold today, I grabbed my naked arms to keep some of the chill away.

"I think you should come with me," he spoke. My hair whipped in my face caused by the wind and I tucked it behind my ears. I stared at him, confused.

"I don't understand."

"You do." He turned slightly, staring at me from the corner of his eyes, studying my expression like there was an answer there I didn't know about. "I can protect you better if you're with me. And away from everything he can hold against you." I gave him one of my amused looks.

I laughed, shaking my head and placing my arms underneath my breasts. "You can't be serious." My laughed faded when I saw that he wasn't sharing the same feelings. He was serious. I sighed. "Where would we go?"

"To my home."

"Your home? Is it like, not on earth?" I asked stupidly.

"I live just outside the Underworld."

My eyes grew wide. "Isn't that just another word for Hell?" He was absolutely insane.

"Yes," he answered, then sighed when I continued to look at him like he was an alien. "Don't look at me like that. It's not how you imagine it."

"I'm not going anywhere!" I snapped. "I can't. My family is here and everyone I care about. How can I just disappear?"

It was his turn to glare. "They are all in danger, Melanie. They would be safer if you weren't around." I couldn't pretend that what he said hadn't hurt. Because it did. It was what I knew and he knew, but the way he said it, was like a punch in the gut. No, a stab to the heart. "My job is to protect you, not them." I felt even more pain, but that feeling quickly turned to anger the more I listened to him.

I tossed my chin up. "That's all I've ever been to you. A job. You're even crueler than I thought."

"You're the one that made things clear between us. You're the one that made it so." His jaw tightened as he spoke.

I moved toward him, throwing my hands in the air. "So what, I made a choice." The mood grew darker between us, but it was too late to stop anything now. "I thought you would understand." My voice broke a bit, showing vulnerability that I didn't want him to see.

He mocked me with his smile and it was an even bigger mockery for me when my heart raced at his devilish smile. "I never claimed to be understanding."

"I see," I spat those two words out icily as I turned away from him. But it didn't last long before I turned back around and grabbed his shoulders. "I'm staying. I'm not leaving with you," I told him sternly, looking him in the eye. "So, I guess you can keep protecting me or just go kill him."

His head fell back with a laugh until he noticed my blank stare, he arched his eyebrow. "Oh, you're serious?" I nodded and he sighed, pulling away from me. "Fear can't be killed; he is an entity. You can't kill something that's been around almost since the beginning of time." was his answer. I didn't like his answer.

"Then what?" I put my hands on my hips. "I don't wanna die so that he can have more power. And I don't want people to get hurt because of me."

For the first time, his smile seemed genuine. "Are you not afraid?"

"I'm always afraid. I have been my whole life because of him. I just don't want to be controlled by Fear any longer."

He studied me. "You're stronger, Melanie." His hardened features slipped into something beautiful as he gazed at me. Almost like he was admiring a part of me. I tried to ignore the way that made me feel.

"What will it be, Reaper? Will you help me?" The wind seemed to blow toward him in my stead, carrying my words to him. He closed his eyes and let out a deep sigh.

"As if you give me another choice." I smiled at his answer.

He brought me back to the hospital before disappearing into the shadows, watching me in secret because I knew—No, I felt he would never leave my side.

In that moment, it felt like everything was going to be okay.

————————

Only everything was not okay. Another day passed and Ryan still hadn't woke. His dad was only now arriving at the hospital, which made me mad, but it wasn't my place to say anything. Surprisingly, Linda spent most of her time at the hospital, looking like a mother to me for the first time. Things got worse when she informed me that he was sent for another surgery after they found some more bleeding on his brain. I felt sick and nauseous after three days of barely eating. Mom made me go to school the next day. Luckily, it was already Thursday so the week was almost over. She was worried about me missing too much school.

I sent Tess a text letting her know I wouldn't be there until that evening and I drug my sorry butt to school. Tess surprised me by showing up at school. "Hey, I'm surprised you came," I told her.

She shrugged her shoulders. "Waiting at home isn't going to change anything. I think Ryan would rather we went to school instead of hovering over him, ya' know?" I nodded, understanding entirely.

The day went in blur, being close to Tess as everyone constantly talked about her brother was a bit much. I could tell it was stressing her out, but she held it in. I didn't understand how no one could see how much their questions were hurting her. Hurting me, but only I never mattered to these people. I was constantly swept aside. Though I didn't mind.

I ate at lunch knowing that it was time to start eating better again or I would be in the hospital myself. Tess was right, he wouldn't want us acting the way we were lately. Sure enough, the food helped. My headache eased and the dizziness I had been feeling all morning was gone.

But as those things faded, the trouble began. Ghosts started coming through the walls, entering the cafeteria. Not like any ghosts I've seen before. No, these were much creepier. They were similar to the soldier at the cemetery but much worse. They were missing body parts and limbs were dangling, some walked awkwardly, their clothes were ripped and some were even naked, but the naked ones lacked any body parts that made them male or female. What made them the most terrifying were their faces. Or lack of. Their faces looked as if they had been carved out, nothing on the inside either. Only hollowed darkness.

I didn't have to turn around to feel the presence behind me. The dark feeling I got from the thing standing behind me caused me to stiffen in my chair. I turned my head ever so slowly to see what it was. Molly was there standing next to a big hulking male. He was bald, scars marred his face and body adding to the pure violence of him. He was terrifying. Molly drew in her breath. "Vengeance, try not to kill her. Fear wants her alive." He smiled, flashing nasty yellow shark-like teeth. He bent his neck to the side causing it to crunch in a sickening way. Molly disappeared.

As I stood up, I noticed all the hollowed faces were standing still. Their necks snapped back and piercing cries echoed throughout the cafeteria. I fell back in my chair, grabbing my ears with my hands and placing my head between my thighs. It hurt so much, I couldn't even think with the blaring in my head. I felt something trickle from my ears. I tried to raise my head to watch the hollowed faces. No one in the cafeteria seemed to hear it but me.

They finally stopped. I slowly straightened myself in my chair, dropping my hands to my sides. Tess gasped, giving me a worried look. "Melanie, what just happened to you? Oh, God. Your ears are bleeding!" I didn't have time to listen to her, Vengeance laughed behind me. I turned back around to stare at him.

"Did you feel the pain they invoked?" He sneered down at me. "They are my puppets. They feed on revenge. On people's darkest secrets and feelings. When someone—or thing does a wrong, they seek out vengeance. Come, human. Now they shall feed on yours." His words were confusing, but still made me worry. Whatever he had just said didn't sound good.

Grim materialized behind the demon, Vengeance. Vengeance must have sensed his presence because he moved faster than my eyes could follow. Grim was right behind him, moving just as fast as he was. Grim's boned hand darted out and his scythe appeared just as he sidestepped in front of Vengeance. The scythe switched into a sword and Vengeance only grinned, whistling in appreciation for the huge sword before his own giant sword appeared. He had the same sort of ability as Grim? I wondered as I watched the two.

"Melanie?" Tess whispered next to me, I

didn't notice the strange look she was giving me. Or anyone else for that matter. They couldn't see what I could. "You're scaring me. What's wrong?" she added.

"Vengeance, I heard you enjoy sword fights most. Shall I show you how to properly use one?" Grim's voice always boomed with power when he was his reaper form. I snapped my head back around to face them, completely ignoring Tess.

"You're baiting me, Grim. Trying to distract me from my prize." Grim's blue glow that always swirled around his bones darkened as Vengeance spoke. "I shall feed on her soul. I'll take that power for myself." Grim tightened his grip on his sword, his blue glow now turned completely black. That emotion must be anger, pure hatred. I sort of guessed at it.

Grim moved forward, aiming his blade at Vengeance. Just before he was close enough, Vengeance jumped in the air. Grim slid his boots against the tiled floor and jumped after him. They collided with their swords in the air. The force of their blow threw them apart from one another. Both landed on their feet and went after one another again. This time, the collision of their swords was stronger. Grim was knocked against the wall, the force of his weight against the wall made a thundering cracking sound in the cafeteria. Everyone quietened. Vengeance fell atop of the cheerleader's table. The table buckled and crumbled to the floor, underneath his weight. The girls screamed, running away from the mysteriously broken table. Everyone looked around the cafeteria confused.

But while everyone was growing worried, the puppets began to move toward every table. They bent down next to every person, whispering in their ears. I had a bad feeling...

Chaos erupted, people started arguing out of nowhere, punches were being thrown, and girls were having cat fights. I looked around completely taken aback. Grim continued to battle with

Vengeance as everyone grew worse. I turned around to my table when I heard Tess smack Mike. I looked at them, shocked and horrified. That's when I noticed the puppet whispering in her ear. He glared at her. "What the hell, Tess?"

Another began to whisper into Mike's. "You fucking man whore. You cheated on me with Haley!" she accused him. I wondered if these arguments were real or the doing of Vengeance's manipulation. The cafeteria was a mad house. Something pressed against my ear.

Grim is to blame.

A voice rattled in my ear. My mind went a little hazy. Huh? He is? Blame for what? I turned around to see one of the puppets standing behind me. It was getting harder to concentrate. My mind felt light and my body heavy.

He knew Ryan was in danger yet he let it happen...

No! I blinked, stunned. That was a lie. Grim wouldn't...

He wanted him out of the picture. It's not you that he wants, it's your power.

The voice slithered and I saw red.

I spotted Grim battling with Vengeance toward the middle of the cafeteria. That's where I stalked, pure malice framing my features. Vengeance was the first to notice me coming and smiled. "Yes!" he roared, pleased with himself. I ignored him though and focused all my hatred on Grim.

Grim stopped his attacks when he noticed me. I couldn't get a read on what he was thinking when he was a skeleton. I stopped once I was in front of him. "Did you know Ryan was going to get hurt?" I asked through clenched teeth.

His body went completely still when I asked him, scaring me more than my thoughts ever did. "Don't listen to his puppets." He tried to walk to me, but I stopped him by holding my hand up between us.

"Don't!" I yelled. "Answer me."

"Yes." He did. He did. He did. I stumbled back in shock and horror. My chest literally felt like it had been ripped open.

"You pretended to care about me because you wanted the power I possessed?" I whimpered, on the verge of tears. Or maybe I was already crying.

He moved forward, extending his boned fingers out to me. "Never." he said without hesitation. I shook my head, unable to believe anything he said.

"No!" I hissed. "Stay away." He froze at my words, hand still extended until it slowly fell to his side. Another evil laugh erupted from Vengeance. "I can't believe I thought you were any different than Fear. Or any of them! You are exactly the same as them. A *monster*." I spat the word in his face, Grim staggered backward actually taken by surprise by my words. It was at that moment Vengeance caught him off guard and sliced open Grim's chest. The blue glow around him began to pour out of his chest wound. Grim grabbed his chest before his glow blackened again as he turned to Vengeance.

"You're foolish. Just as Fear. Like I would actually hand over the Vessel to him?" Vengeance shook his head with a smile before looking my way. I glared at him. He pointed toward me. "All that power is mine to take. Since Fear has her marked, it's almost impossible for any other demon to find her. Luckily, he was stupid enough to show me her whereabouts, of course, thinking I was going to bring her to him." So, he kept me hidden from other demons with the mark he placed on me? I looked around, everyone was oblivious to what was happening. Everyone was in their own battle with one another. I stepped backward, moving away from the two monsters in front of me. I was completely alone.

"That power, you can give it to me *Girl* while I feed on that hatred you are feeling right now." He stalked toward me, my anger dissipated enough that I felt the fear of what's to come. I started to turn, but Grim was in front of me, blocking Vengeance before I got the chance. He grabbed my arm and turned. "We need to leave," his voice was deep, but he also sounded weak. The wound was a funny thing to see on him. He didn't bleed, his blue glow, that I figured might be his own essence, seeped out. Instead of flowing completely out, though, it just seemed to hover there in the air, waiting to be stitched back together. "Your mother is in danger." My heart quickened with more fear. Only I didn't get the chance to ask and he whisked us out of the cafeteria. Then we were standing in my mother's bedroom.

Molly stood above her sleeping body atop the bed with a sinister smile on her lips. "Ah, I was waiting for you." Two figures jumped out from behind us and grabbed Grim. He fell to his knees. I looked down at him surprised. He didn't seem to ever be someone to go down so easily. But he was already injured. Something they held in their hands seemed to hold him in place, it was a black rod that emitted some sort of light against his body, holding him still. He growled angrily as he looked up at Molly.

"Demons are so gullible. Vengeance took the bait just as Fear expected. He was nothing but a distraction. Since you were keeping tabs on everyone she cared about, it made it hard to use them. So, we needed someone to distract you long enough so that we could snatch ole' mommy, and because you were busy with Vengeance, you didn't notice until it was too late. And you even got caught in our trap. What's happened Grim? You're growing weak. Does she have something to do with it?" What did she mean? Was he actually protecting everyone I cared about? My head hurt, I reached for my forehead. No, he was only after my power. She was wrong. Molly noticed his chest and grinned. "He even managed to do some damage, how impressive." It wasn't impressive, not really. It was because he was caught off guard because of me that he was injured. I shook my head.

Grim's whole body seemed to shake with rage and a flicker of worry flashed in Molly's eyes before she masked it. The lights that cast out of the demons' weapons faded, and they looked at them confused before Grim picked himself up and with the roll of his shoulders, tossed them to the ground with a flick of his arms.

Only Molly seemed prepared for him to do that. She pulled out a knife from her dress and bent over Mom's sleeping body. I panicked as the blade pointed against her chest. "Stop!" I yelled.

"Choose. Come with me, your life, for the safety of your mothers. And everyone else you love." Molly gave me a choice; I saw Grim move in the corner of my eye. She did too, she let go of the knife, but the knife still hovered above my mom's chest. "Not so fast, Grim. See, I knew I couldn't hold you off, but it doesn't matter. The knife is spelled, the moment you go after me or the knife, it strikes." Grim stopped next to me. My heart hammered, this was what I planned to do regardless. It just happened sooner than I realized. I nodded, gripping my pants with my hands until my knuckles turned white. This was the way I could protect everyone.

"No." Grim grabbed my arm, but I slipped right through his grip. I didn't even turn to look at him. I wouldn't. No, I didn't want to.

"Okay," I said without hesitation. Molly smiled and with the twirl of her wrist, a huge black portal opened behind her. I watched the knife cautiously as I walked around the bed. She noticed. "The spell will drop on the knife the moment you enter the portal and your mom will be safe. We have no need to harm her as long as you come to him." *Him.* Despite how much I resolved to do this, the thought of being near Fear made my skin crawl.

I nodded. I could feel a change in the room,

313

a shift behind me. "Melanie." Killian was no longer Grim; I could tell by the difference in his voice. I turned my head ever so slightly. His dark eyes seemed to plead with me, in desperation. There it was again, that feeling of being connected to him. So drawn, but it was foolish on my part.

"This has to stop. Nobody else is getting hurt because of me."

I turned my head back around and stepped into the portal.

Chapter Fifteen

I bounced through some sort of never ending tunnel, rays of colors raced against the oval shaped darkness alongside me. Lights that made me think of stars filtered through before I was falling hard onto the ground. The hardened rock below pinched my cheek and scraped alongside my face from the impact. I forced myself to rise slowly, easing myself into a sitting position so that I could see where I was. The first thing I thought was this was some sort of cavern. The caved walls, massive and tall, stretched out above and around me. The granite rock beneath me felt cool to the touch, but everything else seemed to charge with heat. The rock of the walls was gray with black specks through them making the whole place look dark and spooky.

Lanterns that looked as if they had been melted into the cave walls gave a small cast of light. The ceiling felt so far away from where I sat on the ground, making me feel little and afraid of what came next. That's when I noticed the luscious red carpet being rolled out before me. I watched as the carpet rolled and rolled itself until it ended where I sat. I followed the carpet with my eyes to where a huge throne sat empty. I couldn't help but snort. Really? Everything about this place was making me think of some medieval time.

I jumped, standing to my feet when two fountains started spouting out water at the same time. They stood apart from one another, the same as the other, just on opposite sides of the cave. The fountains were made to look like dragons. Both dragon's mouths were tipped upward as if they were spitting fire, only water was what came out. It was lovely, I admit, something mysterious and wary about it. Their wings thrust out from their sides as if they were racing toward the sky. I was admiring them longer than I realized when that admiration turned to horror as the water turned red, as if it were blood.

My whole body chilled and I was reminded of why I was here. Where I was and what I was doing. I shuddered. I couldn't be afraid. I eyed the throne for a minute then began walking across the red carpet. The throne no doubt belonged to Fear. A demon that treated himself as a king, craving more power. It made sense, I felt my mind darken. I felt the fear try to shake me up, cause me to cower, but I couldn't let it. I made a choice. And for me, that choice was the right one. I managed to protect the people I cared about. And I hadn't decided to give up. No, even now as I walked toward the empty throne with no plans or no advantages against such a monster... I wanted to live. But if dying meant protecting the ones I loved then so be it.

I noticed a figure lurking behind the throne.

The throne was tall. It looked as if it was made of bones, as I got closer I realized it *was* bones, forged together to make a giant seat. A gold cloth draped over the seat. I stopped, waiting for the figure to show itself. A little afraid of seeing the thing I've been terrified of for so long. I've imagined so many things in my head of what it would look like. The classroom had been dark, but I knew I felt horns on its head.

"Melanie," a surprisingly pleasant voice called my name behind the throne. I leaned slightly, wanting to see him, also thrown off by the sweet male voice. Then I heard his footsteps as they echoed around the cave, and I watched him move out of the darkness. I couldn't hide my startled face or the gasped that escaped my lips. He was gorgeous. No, he was magnificent. His hair was long and blond, descending his shoulders and back. Crystal blue eyes stared back at me. His features were soft and angelic, nothing like the harsh and rugged beauty of Killian. I shook my head when I realized I was thinking of Killian.

"Who are you?" I asked in disbelief, unable to believe this man could be evil. "You're Fear?" I asked.

His head tilted slightly, his smile overly sweet. Something about it caused goosebumps to run up my flesh. "Are you disappointed?"

The more I learned of demons, the more I realized they were never as they seemed. I sneered at him. "I remember the day you attacked me. I never imagined you to look so *normal.*"

He flung his hair off his shoulder, making it all fall against his back as he moved to the throne and sat down. He circled his wrist around and around before his facade finally dropped. His angelic features hardening, still beautiful but terrifying. "Are you trying to ask if this is what I really look like?" He tilted his chin up. "It is. But I have another form, much like Killian does… Must we start off on the wrong foot?" he asked nicely.

I glared at him. "Oh, I didn't know I was

supposed to forget all the times you tried to kill me. Ryan's in the hospital because of you. And you threatened the life of my mom to get me here."

He held up his hand at me, daring to laugh as my anger continued to fizzle. "Oh, dear. I've made you upset." His laughter died, and once again his facade dropped, showing his lack of emotions. "But you should learn to die the first time," he hissed and I stumbled back. The ground dropped behind me when I did. I jumped forward awkwardly trying to get away from the broken granite below me. I stared down the opened hole and saw the molten lava—I gulped. The heat from the lava blasted me in the face, my hair flew back and I backed away. He sighed and my attention went back to him. "No matter, the power has already awakened thanks to Grim. I should thank him; it makes things easier."

"What are you talking about?" I kept my focus on both him and the lava behind me.

"Ah," he said dramatically. "You don't

know."

"If I knew what you were talking about, would I be asking?" I said, irritated.

"Your feelings toward Grim, what are they?" His question caught me off guard. Without meaning to, I found myself thinking of my feelings.

Then I realized my mistake, I spent too much time thinking of my answer confirming his suspicion. "What are you talking about?" I said hurriedly.

"You know very well what I'm talking about." I looked away. Molly appeared next to me, staggering until she fell to her knees. She looked horrible. Well, more than usual. She was still dead after all. I wondered if Killian had something to do with her injuries?

"My mom?" I asked, not caring to bother that she was badly hurt.

"She's alive," she replied, voice hoarse and small. I was reminded at that moment that Molly was only a mere child. Well, that wasn't true. She died a child. Who knows how many years she had already spent like this after dying.

"Grim?" Fear tapped his throne's armrest impatiently.

Molly lifted her head to glare at him. "What do you think? He's on a rampage. I barely made it through the portal," she hissed, closing her eyes as she jerked her limping arm and twisted it. I cringed at the popping sound. She moved her arm around, testing to see if she had snapped it back in place. It looked painful, but she stood up and shrugged her tiny shoulders like it was nothing.

"I'm sure he will be paying a visit soon," Fear muttered as his gaze left Molly and went back to me. He moved his hand over his chin and I couldn't believe I was just noticing how long his nails were. They were horrifying, pointed and yellow. Completely unmatched to the rest of his beauty. "While we're waiting, what should we do in the meantime?" I noticed he was talking to me again as his eyes raked over my entire body. I felt sick. "I will be needing that Vessel from you, Melanie, before he arrives."

I felt my whole body burn with anger. "Yes, you've went through a lot of trouble to get it," I added sarcastically.

"Now, how do we go about taking it out?" He pondered on his throne and my stomach churned. Oh, yeah. How did that happen? Did I really have to die in order for him to take it? I looked at him nervously.

"How about we just leave it where it's at?" I tried rather lamely. He tilted his head.

"Molly, show her to the bedroom." Fear's eyes never left mine as he spoke to Molly.

I looked toward Molly, trying to hide my fear. *Calm yourself.* I came here knowing that I would probably die. But why did I need to go to a bedroom? All these horrible thoughts kept filtering through my mind. I suddenly felt light-headed and shaky. Not good, I was psyching myself out. I couldn't move, but Molly shoved me to the left. That got my feet moving, but didn't help that she dragged me toward the wooden door embedded into the cave wall. She brought me straight into a bedroom. A wooden bed was at the center of the room. Red silk spilled over the side. But that was where the pretty part ended, creatures hung on the walls, ones I had never seen before or thought to exist. Their eyes felt like they followed me as we entered the room. One giant, black beast's mouth was stretched open as if it was about to attack. I could still smell their evil stench as if they were still alive. A desk sat toward the back of the room, wooden and piled with papers. Molly led me to the bed and forced me to sit.

I clamped my hands and legs together. "What's he going to do to me?" I found the nerve to ask her.

She turned away from me and headed toward the door. She wasn't going to answer me. "Fear will find a way to take the Vessel from you." She stopped walking and sighed as she looked to the ground. I couldn't see her face, but I wondered for a moment what she could be thinking. "Then you are gonna wish he'd just kill you because death is sure to be merciful compared to what he will do to you." She started walking again, slipping out the door. It shut behind her.

Molly's words alone fueled me with an urgency to do something. I tried to leave the room the moment she left but I couldn't. The door must be locked from the other side. I banged and twisted on the door grunting as I did so, but it never budged.

I started searching around the room, avoiding the mounts on the wall as best I could. The nasty glint of the beast's teeth seemed to look bigger every time I looked back at it. One looked slimy and gross, like it might be some sort of water dweller. Like the rest of the cave, the walls were stone even in the room. I slid my hands along the walls hoping for some sort of secret passage. I even looked under the bed and when I spotted a mirror I hadn't noticed before I ran to it, pressing my palm against the glass hoping by some miracle I could walk through. Of course, I couldn't.

"This isn't a movie, what am I expecting?" I grumbled to myself, panic causing my heart to pound and roar into my ears. I could do nothing. I was stuck here until someone came and got me. I grabbed my forehead and tried to even out my breathing.

I stared at my reflection. My jaw was skinned up and red from falling out of the portal. I looked hopeless, really. I could even see the doom in my eyes. It made me think of Mom and Alex and letting myself think of them made me want to cry. I hated to think that they would never even know what happened to me. How long would it take before she realized I was missing? I got on my knees and twirled around on my butt until my back was pressed against the mirror. Mom would be devastated. Ryan and Tess also. I wouldn't even get to be there when he woke up. He was going to wake up knowing everything. He was going to be worried. No, he would be the only person that knew the truth. It would haunt him.

I didn't have time to worry about them, though. I was in real danger. I was pretty sure Killian said something about Fear being unable to take the Vessel from me by killing me now that it had awakened. But he would find a way. I hated to think of what will happen to me once he did.

My thoughts lingered to Killian. He would most likely come to my rescue, but it wouldn't be me that he was coming for, right? It was the Vessel. He was no different than the others. No matter how I might had felt about him it didn't matter when I was only being tricked. When I thought of his betrayal, it hurt so much that I had to grab my chest. Maybe I still didn't want to believe that he betrayed me. Maybe I wanted him to care for me.

Just me.

But I could never forgive him for knowing that Ryan was in danger and doing nothing. Saying nothing.

The wooden door opened and I stood quickly. A strange looking creature walked in. Tiny and odd, I found myself tilting my head trying to figure out what the heck it could be. Three more walked in, all four of them barely came up to my knees. Even though they were small, they were ugly and gross looking. The one in front beckoned the others with its hand to come toward me. I found myself stepping backwards. That one seemed to be in charge as he hissed at the others as if he were hurrying them. Their teeth were white and block-shaped instead of pointy like so many other demons were. They were hairless and shiny looking as they bounced and waddled toward me—their legs were too small to walk normally. "What in the world are you? Stay away!" I shooed them away with my hands. They continued and I found myself standing on the bed to get away from them. I stared at them below me. Two snickered and pointed at me. Obviously I was hilarious.

"They're goblins. Nasty little creatures." I followed Molly's voice to where she stood in the doorway. She looked at the goblins in disgust.

"What do they want with me?" I asked. One tried to climb the bed and I kicked him in the head with my shoe. He flew back a couple feet. The others gathered around their friends checking on him. Once they knew he was okay, they all turned and hissed at me.

"Easy there," Molly warned me. "You don't want to upset them. They are only here to do their job." She flicked a part of her dark hair off her shoulder.

"Job?" I didn't like the sound of that.

She nodded, leaving the doorway and walking into the room. It was always weird dealing with Molly. She looked like a young—although dead, girl yet the way she spoke and carried herself told me she was a lot older. "They are

Dreamkeepers. They can see your dreams as well as create them." And they were going to do something to me? I swallowed nervously. "Lie down and relax Melanie. You are going to be dreaming soon."

All four of them were climbing the bed. I looked to her. "I don't understand. I thought he was taking the Vessel. Why do I need to dream?" I asked unsure.

Molly grinned. "Don't play coy with me. When your power first awakened, what were you doing? More like, what were you dreaming?" She batted her eyes at me knowingly. I blushed. How did she know that? Images from the dream filtered through my mind of Killian between my legs.

Oh, dear Lord.

I didn't understand how that was important. Did he plan to embarrass me to death before taking the Vessel out?

"What does that have to do with the Vessel?" I asked.

"Because the dream is what woke the Vessel. In order for the Vessel to leave your body we need to bring it closer to the surface." Two of the goblins latched onto both my legs, flipping them out from underneath me. They were stronger than they looked. I fell against the silk material on the mattress. When I tried to raise up, the other two were already at my arms. They pinned me down. Molly stood next to the bed. "Honestly, I'm not sure what Fear is thinking," Molly muttered, unsure if she was talking to me or herself I didn't reply.

"Are you going to tell me what the dream was about?" She tilted her head over mine. I looked away which caused her to laugh. "No matter, the goblins will figure it out." She turned to the goblins and gave them a quick nod before walking away. One of the goblins jumped on my chest.

It startled me and I tried to move away. The goblin walked up my chest and bent over in my face. His slimy green hands ran across my face.

I drifted asleep.

There's a knock on the door as I was getting a glass of water in the kitchen. I looked to the clock on the stove, it's two in the morning, who in the world would be at the door this late? I set the glass down and walked into the hallway. There was a knock again before I got a chance to open it. Ryan gave me a lopsided grin when I opened the door. I gave him a look of worry, thinking something must be wrong for him to be here so late. "Ryan? What's wrong? What are you doing here so late?"

He shrugged his shoulders, still smiling. "I just needed to see you."

I just gave him a dumbfounded look. "Okay," I said slowly.

He looked like he was waiting on me to say something else before he finally asked, "Are you going to let me in?"

I nodded my head. "Yeah, of course." I moved to the side and he slipped by me, I noticed how he lingered next to me several seconds too long before walking the rest of the way through the door. Mom was working tonight and Alex was sound asleep in his room.

"Are you sure everything's okay?" I asked again.

He turned around and smiled. "Just wanted to see you." I looked down, the way he was acting had me feeling shy. It was becoming clear that he was telling the truth. He just wanted to see me. My stomach fluttered. It was two in the morning, just how bold was Ryan getting? I knew he cared about me, but this was different.

"You should come over during the day, Ryan. It's two in the morning," I clarified.

He ignored me, I followed him into the living room where he sat down on the couch. He propped his left shoulder back and used his right hand to pat the cushion next to him. "Come over here."

I did as he asked, nerves in my throat. I couldn't bring myself to look at him, afraid of what

I might see. I turned on the TV. The light of the TV was bright and it took a few seconds for my eyes to adjust. A random movie played on the screen. His hand found my leg where he slowly ran his fingers over my flesh. I finally looked at him, his face was full of want, something I'd never seen on him before. He was normally a gentleman. Although I didn't mind this either...

I sucked in air when he surprised me by grabbing my legs and placing them over his. His arm that rested on the couch grabbed my shoulders and pulled me close. I closed my eyes and breathed in the smell of him.

"I don't want to be friends anymore. We've been wanting more from each other for a long time now, Melanie. Let's not fight it," he whispered in my ear, I nodded feeling high on our truth. I couldn't remember how many times I imagined kissing his lips, him holding me like he was now. I always longed for this, but everything was wrong in my life. That didn't matter right now, though.

Ghosts and all my troubles didn't exist right now. For some reason, I couldn't find myself to care at all. I finally had what I wanted.

When his lips grazed mine, I opened my eyes in surprise. This was what I've always wanted, my thoughts melted away and my eyes closed. I pressed my mouth harder into his. His hand found my back where he pressed me into him, I clung to him harder. He parted his mouth slightly, I repeated his movement and soon our tongues were meeting. I sighed in content.

This was nice.

But I wanted more. His hand went lower down my back. Hmm, I kept waiting for something, I wasn't sure what it was. I whimpered in frustration. He continued to kiss me, I opened my eyes. He was so breathtaking, his eyes were closed as he continued to rake his tongue in my mouth, but....

What was missing?

My brain scrambled. A voice filtered through

the fog.

"Wrong person, idiots. Change him!" A man roared, I blinked, breaking our kiss, confused. I looked around the room.

"What's wrong?" he whispered, sounding out of breath.

"What are you doing?" a deep rumbling voice came from the living room entrance. I jumped out of Ryan's lap in a hurry. I pulled down my shorts that were running up my crack and turned around. A huge man lurked slightly in the hallway, shadowed in the darkness, but I could see his eyes sweep over my body. My breath caught, the tall stranger noticed and I let the air escape my lips. I turned to Ryan, but he was gone.

But my thoughts didn't let me get confused, my gaze shifted back to the man. For some reason, I felt different in his presence, his appearance alone seemed to draw out some strange feeling within me. My whole body heated as he stalked closer, his dark eyes moving through the darkness,

roaming over my body. "I asked you a question,"
his voice, both wicked and pure delight, tempted
my ears. I wasn't sure whether to be afraid or just
run into his arms. Both thoughts crossed my mind.

"This is my house. Wh-what are you doing
here?" I somehow managed to speak.

"I know." His hand grabbed the strap of my
tank top. His curled one finger beneath the tiny
strap. That one simple act caused a wave of
pleasure to wash over my body. "I'm here now,
what do you want me to do?" he asked huskily.

I just looked up at him confused, unsure what
he meant. "I don't know." I wrinkled my nose at
him. "Who are you?"

He lowered his head, his chest moving into
my face as he whispered into my ear, "You know
who I am, Melanie." The heat of his breath
caressed my ear.

His hands found my waist, pushing me back
until my heels hit the bottom of the couch. I saw his
cocky grin just as he caught me. He then twisted

my body around, pressing my knees onto the couch. My head ended up pressed against the top cushion. His presence lurking behind me only seemed to fuel my excitement. He pressed against my backside and a shiver rippled through me.

I didn't care about anything. Not even how wrong this was. Only he could make me feel like this. I turned my head to look at him. Desire washed over his features. Desire he had for me. I watched as his eyes roamed over my buttocks before reaching his hand out to do the exact same thing he had been doing with his eyes. I pressed my butt into his palm, instinctively. That caused him to smile, but I could only think of how big his hands were against me.

"Melanie." he moaned my name, his control slipping enough to see something tender beneath the surface. Between us. It disappeared before I got a chance to question it, his control sliding back into its place. In one swift jerk, my shorts were dropped to my knees. My face flushed with heat, I

placed my head into the cushion, ashamed that I was burning with desire. Something pooled in my stomach, clenching my insides, making me want something I've never had. My head jerked back to him when I heard the sound of a zipper being tugged down. "What are you doing?" I asked, voice soft yet throaty.

I knew what he was doing. Although I didn't care, I hadn't thought I'd lose my virginity in doggy style. I watched as he jerked his pants down. I wasn't brave enough to look down so I concentrated on his chest. Big and imposing behind me. More of the foreign pleasure moved between my thighs, I felt wet and achy down there. It was amazing. It was torture. "I'm going to fuck you from behind. Ease the ache you've caused between us"

I nodded silently, unable to say anything back to such wicked words. I found myself whimpering, wishing he would hurry. My need for this stranger pushed all other thoughts from my mind. I jerked when I felt his t-shirt graze against my pale flesh. Even though our skin had yet to touch, the ache only grew more intense. I felt mad and out of control. The madness, I knew, was only the desire I had for him. "Please," I whimpered, looking up to see his face. His hand went to my shoulder. He pushed me back against him until my face was pressed against his. The contact was amazing, such a simple touch left me in flames. He claimed my mouth and I felt myself melt into him, completely. I placed my hand back, grabbing his jaw. I wanted more. His hand slid over my stomach, flaring every nerve to life. His hand slid further down until he was pressing his fingers against my sex. He found my tiny bud and pressed against it.

"Say my name." He bit into my lips as he kissed me.

I knew exactly who he was. I broke our kiss for the tiniest moment so that I could stare into the depth of his dark eyes. "Killian." I replied softly, maybe even a little shy. He took his name on my lips and kissed me with fierce passion and I knew it was everything I craved. Everything I wanted.

I came apart when his finger found my entrance and pressed inside.

I woke to find Fear's hand stretching over my glowing abdomen. I shrieked and pushed him away causing myself to fall back onto the bed. I must had been floating again. My skin was glowing even brighter than it did the first time it happened. Fear growled. He gripped my arms as he began to take huge gulps of air, sucking in the glow from my body. I watched it travel off my skin and into his mouth. The goblins moved off the bed and cowered away from us. Fear held me firm. I looked as his mouth stretched abnormally in front of me taking in the glow. I watched him nervously. Was he really taking the Vessel? Something tugged at my heartstrings at the thought of losing it. His gripped tightened on my arms before he started coughing and choking. Soon the glow he had swallowed came flowing through the air back to me. He staggered backwards, grabbing his throat as if it burnt and looked to me accusingly.

I looked down as the glow faded back into my skin. Fear came after me. He clamped his hands over my neck lifting me off the bed. I placed my hands over his trying to suck in air through my lungs. I couldn't. My throat burned and tightened. I clawed at his hands. I couldn't breathe, he was choking me! I tried reaching for his neck, but the more I tried the further his hands seemed to stretch me away from him. Were his arms growing longer? I couldn't think… my vision blurred and spots began to cloud my vision. I was dying...I had to do something. Panic raced along my veins. I didn't want to die.

One of his hands left my neck, it was then that I was able to suck in a tiny bit of air. I gulped loudly and his gripped tightened once more. His free hand moved toward my chest—his sharp claws aimed. His hand shot out to my chest. I didn't have time to close my eyes. I was watching my own death. I was surprised when his hand went straight through me as if I were a ghost. Fear couldn't hide his surprise and his face grew more irritated as he took out his hand and tried again. The same thing happened. His hand moved through me. I didn't even feel it. He roared and threw me across the room. My body slammed against the rock wall almost hitting one of his mounts. I cried out as the pain raced through my body. It was hard to breathe. I laid on the floor, not wanting to move a muscle until the pain slowed into a dull ache. I slowly stood up.

Fear was raging on the other side of the room. His hands in fists as he glared at me. Something was wrong. He couldn't get the Vessel. I smiled in triumph at him. It caused his anger to increase.

His face seemed to warp for a moment, his teeth lengthened, and his blond hair turned jet black. Horns jutted out of his head before disappearing again. He sucked in a breath and calmed himself as if he were fighting to stay in one form. He finally managed to get himself under control.

His head snapped to the door as Molly walked in. She propped her arms against her chests as she looked at Fear. "The goblins informed me you failed to take the Vessel."

He stalked over to her. "The Vessel has taken with her." She looked to me surprised.

"And you've already tried to kill her?" she asked so immediately that I glared at her. My death was so easily talked about around here.

The corners of his lips twitched, her question only fueled his anger once again. "It seems... it's protecting her." He gritted the words out, his voice warped with fury and disappointment. That made sense. No wonder he was so upset. He tried to kill me but couldn't. Maybe I could survive somehow if the Vessel was keeping me safe.

Molly didn't seem so upset—her expression

was blank. "There's another problem." She got his attention once again. When he finally looked back up to her she continued, "Grim was spotted on the outskirts of the Underworld. He won't be long now."

That made Fear smile. It was a smile I didn't like. "Excellent. We've been waiting." He turned to me still smiling. I glared back. "Get our guest ready for our company," he ordered Molly before walking out the door. She nodded as he left. ``

Why did I have such an ominous feeling?

CHAPTER SIXTEEN

I was forced to wear a white silky dress that clung to my body. It brought out the curve of my hips that I never realized I had. I stared at my reflection in the mirror—at least my boobs were covered, but the round curve of them still pressed against the dress somehow made me feel exposed. I glared at Molly behind me through the mirror. Why was Fear dressing me up? I didn't understand the way his twisted mind worked. Just what was he planning?

I noticed a hint of something in Molly's expression as she watched me. I studied her… what was it? Was it envy? Or longing? I decided I didn't care to bother with her thoughts. She was the blame just as much as he was. "Why do I have to play dress up?" I sighed, looking away from the mirror and at her.

She let out a long sigh before answering, "Fear loves entertainment. Or games, more like. I'm afraid you are the entertainment."

I figured as much. I looked to her blood-stained clothes suddenly wondering. "Since you're not exactly a ghost anymore can't you change your clothes?" I asked. She responded immediately with a harsh growl, grabbing her blood-stained dress and crumbling it up in her tiny hands.

"Bummer," I nettled her. She looked as if she wanted to hurl something at me, but she took a deep breath and decided not to. Looked like I found something to aggravate her with. I had to make sure to bring it up around her more. It felt wrong to pick on a child, but she wasn't one. She was probably a lot older than me. Not to mention she was the reason I was here. She helped Fear although I didn't understand why. She seemed to hate him as much as I did.

"No kidding," she finally replied, twirling on her feet walking to the door. "Let's go."

I followed behind her as she led me back into the throne room. The red carpet was gone, replaced with a long rectangle table several feet in front of the throne. A red table cloth stretched over the entire length of the table—it was only when I was closer to the table that I noticed the cloth looked scaly. It tempted me to run my fingers across it; it was rough and bumpy.

"Take a seat." Molly pulled out a chair for me to sit at the far end of the table.

"Are we eating?" I asked nervously. The idea of having to eat anything he offered made my stomach queasy. There was no way I was eating anything.

"Who knows," she grunted behind me before walking away. She disappeared into the dark shadows of the room. I sighed and looked around anxiously. Both dragon fountains still ran red. I noticed someone walking out of the shadows.

Fear ditched his pants and shirt from earlier, replacing them with black and red kimono that lay open partly at the top exposing his pale skin. His chest was hairless—flawless even. "You look lovely for someone so evil," I spat the words out. It only seemed to please him. He took a seat at the opposite end of the table from me. I was glad he chose to stay far away from me.

"I see that you're wearing the gown I sent for you." I rolled my eyes. As if he gave me a choice. He leaned down and looked underneath the table. I knew he was staring at my legs. I covered my bare knees with my hands not wanting him to see any part of me. "The dress belonged to one of my late wives. She was a lovely woman, that is," his voice grew darker, "before I had to kill her for trying to escape." I must have given him a wide-eyed looked because he tossed his head back and laughed. He was insane.

I wasn't sure if that was meant as a real threat or a way to frighten me more. I swallowed—my throat felt heavy and dry. I needed to calm down. Really... how was that possible? No, it was obvious he couldn't kill me like he planned or I would already be dead when he had tried earlier.

With a snap of his fingers, servants started coming out with plates in their hand. I looked around wondering where they came from. I only saw the door to the bedroom. Maybe there were other doors lurking in the darkness? The lanterns weren't lit and the cave walls were covered in darkness. All that lit the room was some sort of light cast over the table. I wasn't sure where the light came from, it was just there. One of the servants had red skin, but other than that he looked normal. Another came out completely covered in hair, I couldn't even see a face. No eyes or ears, only a snout that stuck out through the long hair. I assumed that thing was a male since he wore the same attire as the red skinned male. His hair spilled out of a white shirt and hung over the top of his pants. It was gross. Two females came out and

I had to look twice to make sure I was seeing right. One was red skinned, but the other female was half a horse. The top half of her was completely normal until I looked at her torso and saw the rest of her body shaped into a horse. Brown furry body, legs, hoofs, and a swaying tail hanging in the back.

She slammed the plate down in front of me and I snapped my neck up to see her angry scowl. "Stop staring, it's rude."

I looked down quickly, feeling my face go hot. I didn't mean to offend her, but she was so strange to look at. "Don't mind her, Elise. She doesn't have your beauty." He stared at her rump— expression full of lust. I was going to hurl.

I hid the disgust from my face. She gave him a bright smile and winked. He eyed *all* of her up and down. "Shall I come to you tonight?" she asked, her voice full of hope and want.

"I'll be waiting." He tipped his head back at her with a smile before returning his focus on me. "Do you wish to join us?" He was staring directly at me. I wished he hadn't been, so that I could pretend that question hadn't been directed to me.

"You make me sick," I snarled.

The hairy male guy, thing—whatever he was, began taking the lids off the dishes. I looked in horror—trying to keep my mouth from falling open as a hand started crawling toward me. I stood up. "Sit back down," Fear ordered and the tone of his voice told me not to dare disobey. I slowly sat back down trying to inch away from the hand that was coming toward me.

I noticed another dish was a tentacle still flopping around as if it was alive. The dish beside the tentacle almost looked normal despite the bright color of the meat and veggies. I had a feeling it wasn't anything I wanted to know about. I heard Fear across the table slurping on something. I heard a crunch. I cringed, but didn't dare look up to see what he was eating.

The hand jumped in my lap and I tried to toss it off, but it kept latching onto my dress every time

I did. I held my dress down as the hand tried to go underneath it—between my legs. A sick feeling shot in my stomach. "Leave it be. It's your companion for tonight." I shuddered. He looked amused. This was worse than being killed. This was exactly how he planned to torment me. I finally got a good grip on the hand and tossed it in the floor. I lifted my head up and glared at Fear. "Would you rather it be Grim's hand instead?" I ignored him knowing he was only trying to get a reaction from me. "Oh no?" he added, twirling his finger in the air while smiling. "Or better yet, it's Killian, right? The one you fancy?"

"What are you getting at?" I clenched my teeth.

"What? Are your feelings for Grim amusing to you as it is for me?" He tilted his chin up to mock me.

"I could care less about him," I answered. I felt a trickle of sweat coat my skin. Maybe I could believe my own lies if I kept repeating them.

He shook his head. His razor-sharp nails waving back and forth in the air irritating the heck out of me as he moved his hand around in front of his face. "You lie. You care a great deal about the Reaper."

"I still don't know what you're talking about." I squirmed in my chair, wishing this conversation would end. I didn't like how much Fear noticed. The hand was climbing my foot and I kicked it away.

The red skinned female brought out two wine glasses and brought one to each of us. She poured something green in them. I wrinkled my nose in disgust.

"You can't lie to me, Melanie. I know everyone's fears and weaknesses. Especially yours, I feed on them." He closed his eyes and licked his lips. "The fear you carry always smells so delectable." He sniffed the air in front of him and my skin was a crawling. "You grow afraid of your feelings for Grim. You have no control over it.

You feel shame and guilt when you think of the human boy," he tilted his head in the air trying to remember something. "Ryan, that's his name. You feel guilty for having thoughts about Grim knowing the boy loves you."

"Enough!" I snapped. "You don't know anything." But the voice in my head whispered, *he knows everything.*

He only grinned. "No need to look at me like that." The hand jumped back into my lap and I had to break our eye contact to fight with it. The hand was only causing my anger to boil over until I noticed the fork. I quickly grabbed the hand, placing it on the table then I picked up the fork and stabbed the sucker to the table. It wiggled and wormed, but I dug deeper into its flesh until it stopped moving. I sighed in some relief.

"That was uncalled for." Fear looked to the hand in pity.

"Should have kept its hand to itself," I said staring at the hand.

I caught Fear's smile from the corner of my eye. I didn't like the way he was looking at me. I glanced up at him. "I believe we keep getting off on the wrong start." He smiled gently and my skin tingled in discomfort.

My smile was not so sweet. "I believe that's an understatement."

"It doesn't have to be this way." Was he trying to play a trick on me? I wouldn't fall for anything he said.

"You made it this way."

"Stay here as a guest until the Vessel is mine and you have my word that I won't harm you."

I rolled my eyes. "I'm not stupid enough to believe anything you say. The truth is, you can't hurt me, right? You already tried to kill me and failed." His eyes crystallized and I knew I should stop talking, but I couldn't will myself to. "I don't need to fear you anymore, Fear. You can't hurt me," I mocked.

He took a sip of the green colored stuff in the

wine glass before sneering at me. "That's where you are very, very wrong." My lips curled out. "You see, I'll admit I don't believe I can harm you. But that doesn't mean there aren't other ways." I went still at his words. What did he mean? Was I wrong?

"You see... I can't kill you myself, but what's to say you won't die of natural causes. Such as... drowning from liquid going down the wrong pipe." He pointed to the glass of the green liquid inside. "Drink," he ordered me.

I didn't. I wouldn't. I shook my head. "Don't make me angry," he added bitterly. I eyed the green liquid with suspicion before I grabbed it and took a drink. It was bitter and warm—nasty in my mouth. I spat it back out immediately. He laughed as he took another drink of his. He was messing with me.

"No worries, you're nothing but a human. You won't live forever. You will eventually die and once you do your soul will come to me." He pointed at the mark on my chest and I grabbed it instinctively. The mark fired to life and danced its pain onto my skin. He grinned. "The Vessel will be mine because you belong to me Melanie. Whether you die tonight or sixty years from now. Your soul will come to me and it will be here, where you will be trapped for all eternity." I couldn't shake off the dread I felt at his words.

Something exploded behind me.

CHAPTER SEVENTEEN

"I see our guest has finally arrived," Fear spoke aloud

I whipped my head around to see Killian standing—shoulders tensed, looking lethal and frightening. He stood next to the crumbled cave entrance he made himself. Shattered rocks scattered at his feet as more continued to tumble off the destroyed cave wall. Relief spread through my chest at the sight of him. *He came for me,* my heart thumped. *He came for the Vessel*, the bitter part of me whispered. Still, I moved from the chair, but the armrest shot out around my arms turning into hands that held me to the chair. The arms snaked themselves around my abdomen and back, wrapping themselves around and around the back of the chair where they traveled to my legs and did the same thing. My arms were trapped in the process and I couldn't even wiggle. I had no room to move whatsoever.

"You didn't have to destroy my cave. I do have a door," Fear added nonchalantly, clasping his hands together on the table before smiling.

I tried to turn my head around to see what Killian was doing, but the chair held me exactly how Fear wanted me. As if the chair could read my mind—it twisted around so that I could see him. His eyes found mine immediately—softening, just knowing that I was okay before darkening as his gaze swept over my trapped body. His shoulders went taut. He looked even scarier than he did when he entered. Killian neck made a sickening pop as tilted it to the side. He looked crazy—*delirious* even—as he looked at me. The sound caused me to flinch. The chair decided to move again and I was being pulled backward with the chair and slid to the side before coming to a stop next to Fear.

Killian's fury seemed to heat the entire room but Fear only smiled. He was playing with him. Killian was too upset to take notice.

"Are you okay?" Killian voice came out harsh and cold but I knew it wasn't directly toward me. I gave him a quick nod. His attention shifted back to Fear. "Don't worry, I came to take you home." Only he wasn't looking at me when he spoke. His eyes were challenging Fear.

Fear dropped his hands and leaned back into his chair. The chair's grip on me tightened. I hissed in pain trying to suck air in and out like I was supposed to, but my ribs felt like they were going to shatter. I sucked in trying to lessen the pain. I felt my eyebrows bunch together and I squeezed my eyes shut trying hard not to focus on the pain.

"Stop!" Killian roared.

"But, I'm having so much fun."

The chair loosened its grip on me. My face fell over in my lap as I sagged in relief regaining some of the oxygen I had lost. "You're no match for me, Marcus. Do you really wish for us to fight?" Killian's deep voice crackled in the cave.

I raised my head tilting it slightly so that I could see Fear. His expression soured. "Marcus." He laughed. "You haven't called me that in a long time."

"How did you become this way?" Killian asked.

"It comes with the name." Fear shrugged his shoulders.

"You have no need for her."

"I do," Fear replied quickly. "As you just reminded me, I need the Vessel. I am meant to be more than you." He truly hated Killian. The way he looked at him worried me.

Killian shook his head. "So that's what this is all about." Killian looked to him disappointed. Fear's face burned with resentment. "Foolish demon." I felt like this wasn't about me anymore. There was something between them that I didn't know about. What exactly happened between them?

Killian began to shimmer—fading in and out until Grim finally took his place. Grim's hand stretched before him where his scythe appeared. Fear rose from his chair—stretching his arms out wide. A dark smile crept over his lips. "Finally who I've been waiting for." Fear kicked the table, it slid toward Grim. Grim jumped onto the table as it moved, walking toward us as it continued moving in the opposite direction. Once he was at the other end, he jumped off. He was going to Fear.

Fear slipped off his kimono. I was glad to see he had dark silk pants on underneath. His white skin glowed in the dark as he bared his chest. His body began to change shape and form—like the way Killian did before becoming Grim. The beauty of his face was the first to leave him, stripping away, exposing the monster he truly was. His teeth lengthened becoming sharp and pointed at its tips.

His eyes turned a crimson shade of red as his blond hair turned jet black. His ears disappeared dissolving into his skin, blending in as if he didn't have any. Two horns grew out of his hair that curved backwards. His long nails darkened turning into something that looked more like weapons.

I trembled. The last to appear was his long tail that slipped out of the back of his pants. It was as long as his body—maybe longer and thick and black like his hair. My heart was pounding against my rib cage as I stared at him. Only I wasn't staring at him any longer. I was back in the classroom. In that dark place, alone and afraid as he pinned me down to the ground and marked me, causing me to hate my life after that.

I was in a nightmare. A horrible nightmare. I never saw him that day, but now I was right next to him. The very thing I was most afraid of. And I was afraid. Really, truly, afraid. I watched as he whipped his tail around to his side. I was no different than the nine-year-old stuck in the classroom. I felt clammy and sick, out of motion, like I wasn't even in time. I was just stuck somewhere in between.

His attention was directed at Grim. I stared at the pale nightmare with beautiful hair and terrifying eyes. Grim's scythe transformed into a double-bladed sword momentarily taking my thoughts from Fear. Then they were jumping in the air simultaneously. One blade held over his head as the other aimed at Fear. He met him in the air. Before he was even close enough to use his blade, Fear's tail whipped out from behind him grabbing Grim's ankle and slamming him to the ground.

Grim was back on his feet already going after him again. He moved quicker this time. Fear stood on the ground—anticipating his move—right before Grim's sword struck, but a sword materialized in Fear's hand.

So, I guess it wasn't that big a deal that Grim could change his weapon when all the other demons could do similar tricks as well. They clashed swords over and over causing the cave to echo with a thundering response. Neither was making any direct hits; it was as if they were just bouncing around one another.

"Really? Sword fighting again? Aren't you the Grim Reaper, can't you do something cooler?" I found myself yelling across the room at Grim. I wanted to sound motivational, but somehow ended up sounding rude. He snapped his head around quickly, so did Fear. His blue essence around him seemed to brighten and grow out before darkening. I stumbled back, did I really just say that? What if he got mad and decided to leave me here? *No, he did still want something from me...* I thought miserably.

Something began to rumble beneath my feet. I stared down at my feet—still stuck in the chair. The ground rumbled again, shaking the entire cave. I looked around at the cave walls, its strength buckled under the pressure. Oh, God. What was happening? What if the cave collapsed? That would be a horrible way to die. I looked up at the ceiling warily, hoping it would stay right where it was. But the ground several feet in front of me began to fall into a small hole, that continued to expand—rippling further out. The hole was enormous now and almost at my feet, I would fall in! I pushed my feet to the ground trying to create leverage against the chair, but I had none. My body never budged underneath the chair's hold. "Stupid chair!" I hissed. My hair was falling in my face, but I couldn't even move it out of the way.

A weird sound poured out of the opening in the ground. I stopped fighting against the chair and froze. It sounded like some sort of animal. A roar... I hoped not. Some sort of mating call? Whatever it was… I prayed it stayed down below. Then I heard movement inside the hole like maybe whatever was down there was coming up. The hole was dark and I couldn't see anything that was inside, but maybe that was a good thing. Giant claws snaked out. Or was that talons? Its claw was as big as me.

Then the rest of it glided out. The creature was massive and long. When the full body came into view I knew exactly what it was.

Dragon.

Its skin looked leathery from its scales, but also shiny and brown colored—almost slimy looking. Its face came into view when it twisted its body around to face me. The face was bigger than me and wider—red hair spiked the top of his head and on its chin. Jutting sharp points framed the dragon's face making the beast even scarier looking. Yellow eyes locked on mine and a tiny tongue slithered out. The dragon had no wings, but I was sure it was still a dragon. I meant, not all of them had to have wings, right? When the last of its tail came out of the massive hole in the ground it began to close back up.

With the hole gone, the dragon paced toward me. I looked to Grim who was locked in swords with Fear bouncing all over the cave walls. I had never seen a fight anything like the way these demons do. But I didn't have time for thoughts like that. Grim should have realized the dragon. The dragon only grew nearer so I screamed. "Grim!" He jumped away from Fear, swiveling his head around to look at me. Fear jumped him and I was sure my distraction was going to get him hurt, but he blocked Fear's attack right before he could slice his shoulder. I sighed in relief, but the dragon was already in front of me. The dragon blocked my view of Killian. The dragon scooped me up in its claw—still in the chair—and moved me to its face. Its breath blew out of its nostrils blowing my hair back. I blinked—the stench burnt my eyes. Its talons curled around the chair, squeezing tight. Grim appeared out of the air and attacked its neck. The sword only bounced off the dragon's scales causing Grim to fall back. He caught himself on the ground, stumbling back a few steps before he steadied himself.

"You don't even know what it truly means to be Grim." Fear barked from somewhere in the cave before jumping in to attack Grim from behind. Grim swiveled his body around in time and blocked the sword. The dragon whipped its body around, sliding his tail across the floor catching Grim off guard. His feet flew out from under him, flipping him on his back.

"Grim," I yelled with worry. His eyeless face gave me the briefest glance before hurrying back to his feet. Grim was outnumbered... how was he supposed to handle attacks from both of them? The dragon still gripped me in the chair, but for now its focus was on Grim. I wiggled in the chair feeling completely useless. I couldn't even help myself.

"You never deserved to be Grim," Fear hissed. I studied the demon as his eyes grew redder. The way he spoke made me think he was talking to Killian—not Grim.

Grim gripped his sword, taking his time walking toward him. "You don't deserve to live," his voice rumbled through the cave. His anger with Fear was growing with every word that came out of Fear's mouth.

Swords collided again as they went head on. The dragon drew its head back, taking in a deep breath as it faced Grim. I had a feeling I knew what it was about to do. "Grim, watch out!" I said right before the fire shot from its mouth. My words didn't reach him in time. He wasn't quick enough to dodge the dragon's flames. The force of the hit threw him against the cave wall. He fell to the ground in a mass of flames.

I screamed his name as I stared at his crumbled body. The chair's grip on me suddenly went slack, loosening around me. In a frenzied rushed I got my arms out. I began to shimmy my body up out of the chair's hold as well as the dragon's grip. I was afraid of cutting myself on the dragon's talons, but I tried to ignore that part and concentrated on getting away from the beast. Once my body was out of the chair, I stared down at the ground. The drop to the ground would be dangerous, but I had no other choice. Holding my arms out from my sides—I jumped. The impact on my feet was too strong—I grunted. My knees buckled against my weight. Pain darted up my legs and arms. I winced and hurried to my feet. The dragon realized I escaped from the chair and with a roar—the chair crumbled. I gasped knowing that could have been me. I ran from the dragon. I heard its steps behind me. The cave jarred underneath its weight. I eyed the wooden door that led to the bedroom. It wouldn't be able to reach me in there. I hurried in the direction of the door and stopped when I remembered Grim.

I turned around to see that he was still laying on the ground covered in giant flames. He was rising off the ground, but the flames weren't fading. I didn't even notice that I was running toward him. The dragon was closer to me now that I changed direction. I could hear the wind off the dragon's tail as it moved after me. I looked back to see the tail was moving toward me. If that thing hit me, I wasn't sure I would live through the impact. I stopped running and braced myself for the impact.

Grim appeared and scooped me up in his arms. He jumped up into the air with me just in time. I blinked several times to make sure I was really in his arms. Once I knew, I hooked my arms around his neck as he jumped us around in the room dodging the dragon as he brought us next to the throne. He placed me down and I just looked at him. The flames coated his clothes as if it was never going to burn out. His chest moved with his breath—deeply—in and out. He was tired. I could still see the blue glow leaking out from his wound on his chest that Vengeance caused. It wasn't healed completely yet.

I grabbed his shoulders "You're hurt," I stated the obvious.

He grabbed my hands. There was a gentleness about it that left me confused before he pushed them aside. "I'm fine." I could tell by the strain in his voice that he was lying.

"You're not. Just get us out of here," I told

him. The dragon stomped toward us, shaking the ground as he moved. Grim shifted back into Killian. He grabbed his chest and hunched over from the pain. The fact that he was Killian again was worrisome.

"It's not that simple. He has a barrier spread around the place. Why do you think it took me so long to get to you? No one can use any sort of power to get in or out of this place except him." I nodded to let him know I understood. Remembering Fear, I looked around the cave for him. Where was he? "Besides, he isn't going to stop coming after you, Melanie. I have to stop him," his voice was clouded with anger despite the pain he must be in. His pupils dilated and he gave the dragon a murderous look.

I placed my hand on his chest gently, remembering that he was injured. "What do you plan to do? You're hurt, but you won't admit it."

His hardened features softened when he looked away from the dragon and to me. His hand cupped my left cheek. His eyes found something in mine. I held my breath, the chaos around us seemed to blur in the background. He eyed my lips before his jaw set, his eyes molding—burning itself into my memory. Something about this moment with him had me thinking of words like *Forever*. Which was completely insane. Finally, he said, "I'll be fine. And I'll take you home afterwards and help you fall sleep if you need me to." His touch left my cheek, coldness replaced his warmth. He shifted back into Grim. The blue light around him intensified as he glanced at me once more before moving toward the dragon.

The scythe was already in his hand. He jumped above the dragon's head; I was always stunned at how easily him and every other demon could jump around as if gravity never existed. The dragon tilted his head to look at him. It braced its body, its mouth growing wide as its nostrils flared. The dragon inhaled causing the hair on its chin to move. Grim reared back and roared at the dragon.

Grim's scythe lengthened and turned to a shade of blue. The same color as his essence around him. He lunged for the dragon. The dragon was extremely slow when it came to its body movement because it was so big. It couldn't stop Grim as he pierced its neck. Unlike the first time he attacked the dragon he went through the scaly skin. The dragon screamed in agony as Grim moved the tip of the scythe on down his chest, tearing it open. Black blood fell around them and poured from its chest. The dragon grabbed its chest, roaring one last battle cry before crumbling to the ground.

Grim watched the dragon. Unable to read his expression when he was Grim, I wondered what he was thinking. Something murky and black floated above the dragon and traveled into his scythe. That seemed to happen every time he took a life.

Someone clapped next to me. I turned to see Fear clapping as he sat on his throne. "That's more like it, Grim." His eyes are looking at Grim with nothing but appraisal. Grim was already moving toward us. I started backing away slowly—never taking my eyes off Fear. I wanted as far away from him as I could get. "Not so fast." His red eyes, the ones that were giving Grim a look of approval a moment ago, glared at me. I froze, not sure what I could do.

"It's over, Fear." Grim seemed to carry his power on his shoulders, oozing his hatred toward Fear from his lips—er, bones. A deadly combination that even caused me to get chill bumps. He took slow, sure steps toward the throne. Fear's face lit up with amusement. I wanted to smack that smug look off his nasty face. With the flick of his wrist, something snapped above me. I looked up in time to see a huge cage falling over me. I hunkered down fully expecting it to crush me, but it only trapped me.

I ran to the bars and glared at Fear. "How many more things does he got up his sleeve?" I fumed. I needed to watch when he flicked his wrist. I was learning something bad always happened when he did.

"She'd make a good pet, wouldn't she Grim?" Fear chuckled. Grim tightened his fist around his scythe before his blue essence changed color. The swirling mass of black surrounded him. Something about it was lethal. I took a step away, not sure why I did.

Fear zeroed in on my movement, taking in my fear. I knew because I felt it. He finally looked away from me and back to Grim. "I see I've made you mad." He placed his hand over his chest as he spoke. "Believe me when I tell you, I never wanted to fight with you." Something about the way Fear spoke made me uneasy. The way he looked at Grim—the way he studied him. It was almost like there was some sort of longing. Or some sort of want there. I shook my head. No, that couldn't be right. I meant, he could be into him...

"We don't have to fight if you just hand over Melanie." Grim stopped walking, but the dark mass around him continued to swirl and rage around him.

Fear snorted. "Grim." He nodded. "Tell me it isn't so?" Fear was giving me a weird look before facing Grim again. "You actually have feelings for a *human*?" The word 'human' was spat out of his mouth as if it was vile and disgusting.

Grim went rigid. I dropped my hands to my sides. The black mass grew fainter and fainter as his eyes roamed over me. His shoulders dropped and his attention snapped back to Fear as he had been caught red handed. I looked to Grim confused. Through the opening of his shirt inside the hole of his chest, something flickered. Something real and powerful. Not a heart, more like a feeling... I wondered why I was thinking such strange things. Fear's laugher brought me out of my perplexed state. I was able to look away from Grim and focus on him. Fear shook his head at Grim. "In all my three thousand years, never thought I'd see an entity succumb to a human girl.

A little emotion. I guess, it's big though, for you, that emotion is." Grim still hadn't moved, his black mass flaring back to life around him as Fear spoke. "Take a close look." He was pointing at me. Grim was looking at me—staring so intensely— what was he trying to see? My palms were sweaty. I wiped them alongside the dress I wore feeling self-conscious and nervous. "Does she look like she could love a skeletal being? Hmm?" His words left me in shock. Why was he doing this? "She might have some feelings for Killian but not you." Fear gave me a look of triumph.

Grim was nothing more than a mass of blackness now. I could barely make out his skeletal silhouette. I glared at Fear suddenly afraid of what he was trying to prove. "What are you trying to do?" I scowled at him.

He ignored me, though and kept his focus on Grim. "You were never meant to love. How can you fall for any woman? Or anything for that matter? You were created for one reason and one reason only; to guide the dead to their fate balancing the cycle of good and evil."

"You know not of what I am. Or what I can be," Grim rumbled through the blackness he surrounded himself in. I feared for him. Or *him*. I wasn't sure of my emotions. Fear's words seemed to cut me like a knife.

"Oh," Fear said surprised. "Maybe you think you can love," he acknowledged, but I knew he was purposely trying to anger Grim. I just didn't know why. "She will never love you. She thinks you're nothing more than a monster like me." That caused me to remember the harsh words I said to him before I left through the portal with Molly. I had called him a monster no different than Fear. I hadn't meant it like that. No, I had. I could never change what I said. "Tell him, Melanie. The truth. That you could never love him, only the demon he merged with so long ago." I tried to say something, but no words came out. I wasn't sure what to say.

I waited too long to speak. Grim stepped

forward and was immediately trapped in a circle of light. The black mass of his essence vanished around him—not even the blue glow returned. His hands went to his face trying to shield himself from the bright light that bound him. The circle grew wider, expanding the light around him.

"You walked right into the trap so easily. The girl has truly weakened you. You were so caught up in the truth about her that you failed to sense the magic in front of you," Fear mocked him, rubbing his fingers together. Grim was in pain. He fell to his knees—his body bending back. He grabbed his head. A roar escaped his chest telling me whatever was happening to him hurt. He bucked around on his knees before crumbling to his side twisting and turning.

"Grim!" I called his name, but he couldn't hear me.

"Did I forget to mention that the Vessel wasn't the only thing I was after?" Fear rose from his throne and walked toward Grim trapped in the light. Fear smiled into the circle at him. "You realize what I want Grim? What I have always wanted?" Grim somehow managed to tilt his face up to look at Fear. "You chose Killian over me so long ago. I still don't understand why and can never forgive you for it, but I will soon enough when you and I are finally one," he purred. He planned to merge with Grim? That wasn't possible, was it?

Dread coursed through my veins, making me dizzy with realization. Grim walked straight into a trap when he came to rescue me. "Stop it!" I screamed. "You're hurting him!"

Fear sneered back at me. "No, you're the one that's causing him pain. I will set him free of those feelings once we are merge." I shook my head; Fear was far crazier than I realized. I pulled and kicked at the bars that held me trapped. Grim thrashed around in the light, grunting in pain. I could do nothing. Absolutely nothing.

But the worst part was yet to come. Another

roaring howl tore from Grim's chest and he grabbed his head again— he was back on his knees. Then something happened that confused my mind. Killian was stretching out of Grim— splitting from him. Starting at the head and moving on down to his torso. They were already halfway apart; Killian was holding on to his head the same way Grim was. I knew my mouth was gaping open from the shock. They snapped back together and I was almost positive Fear's plan didn't work. But Killian split right back out separating completely from Grim. They fell to the ground opposite directions of each other. I gasped. It felt so unreal that I was seeing the two of them next to each other. Something wasn't right about it. "Killian!"

Whatever Fear accomplished was bad because he smiled. He turned around. His eyes landed on me. His tail whipped toward the cage and I stumbled back.

I found it hard to breathe, let alone try to think about what just happened. Killian and Grim,

I thought they were always going to be one person after the merge? How could they just split apart? Their trouble caused me panic and confusion. Fear tossed the cage up in the air with his tail. It went flying behind me. I took no time on running away, but I didn't get three steps before his tail snaked out and grabbed my left ankle. I fell to the ground, my chin smacking against the hard ground. Air escaped my lungs in a giant whoosh and for a second I couldn't figure out how to get it back.

"You're still needed." He stepped in front of me and bent down, grabbing a handful of my hair. He yanked me to my feet with it. My scalp was on fire as I hurried to get on my feet to lessen the pain. I kicked my foot out to hit him and he dodged easily. Face hot with rage—I spat in his face. His jaw tightened—his eyes glowing red as he growled at me. I realized the mistake I made.

He let go of my hair and I hurried to gain better footing. I saw his arm rear back and I knew what he was going to do, but I was too slow to stop it. His claws slashed across my chest. I yelled and hissed from the pain. "I wouldn't make me angry. Although, I can't kill you. I can make your life long and miserable." I believed every word he said. I grabbed my chest. It stung so bad. I glanced down to see four slash marks marred across my chest. There was barely anything left of the front of my dress, his razor-sharp nails had torn apart the dress as well as my flesh. The dress was already soaked in my blood; the burning still hadn't stopped. I couldn't even touch it, it hurt so much.

"Melanie," Killian finally came to. His voice was raspy and weak. He was slowly bringing himself to stand on his feet. Grim was picking himself on his knees. The two of them looked at each other for the briefest moment and something passed between them—some sort of understanding before they looked at me.

Killian moved toward the end of the circle. Fear held up his hand. "Careful, Killian. You know what it will mean if you pass over the spell without

Grim. He can't crossover. He will belong to me."

Fear's hand shot out to the back of my neck. His grip was rough as he brought me against him. My back pressed against his bare chest and it made me feel sick and clammy. I was repulsed by him. I thought my body might literally fall apart having to feel his touch. I tilted my head to the side to look at his face. It was something nightmares were made of and this close… I could smell the stench of his wickedness radiating off him as it had its own scent.

Killian glared long and hard before his wrath turned into a mere smile. "You seem to be forgetting something. My job—our job, is to keep Melanie safe and alive. No matter the consequences." Killian looked back at Grim. Grim nodded—there was something between them again. Fear tightened his hold on my neck and grinned at them.

Killian pushed through the barrier of light and the moment he did, the light completely vanished.

No, not vanished. Something bright wrapped around Grim's torso and chest. He could only look down as the bright white chain wrapped and tightened around him. He snapped his neck up to Fear. Something terrifying ripped through his scream. It was anger and raw power.

Killian ran forward—eyes locked on Fear. Fear released my neck and slung me across the floor. My body moved through the air too fast. I couldn't make out what was happening to me until I smacked against the rough ground, tumbling around a few times. Pain tore through the slashes on my chest and into my stomach. When I finally stopped tumbling my body was screaming in protest. I was nauseous and tired. Was I still losing blood? Ignoring my bruised and battered body, I lifted my head up to see Killian's boots running toward me. He knelt beside me and placed his hand on my shoulders to help me off my stomach. I stumbled trying to stand on my feet again, but he was there to catch me, lifting me up until I was firm in his embrace.

My breath caught, whether it was from him or the pain I felt throughout my body—I didn't know. His eyes roamed over my injuries. I swore he looked like he could murder something when he spotted the marks across my chest. "I'm going to kill him," he raged.

I leaned against Killian's broad shoulders trying to see if I could see Fear. I knew it. My eyes widened when I saw that he was walking over to Grim, an evil glint in his eyes. He wanted Grim all along? I pulled away from Killian enough to look at him. I tugged at his shoulders. "He's after Grim."

Killian swore. With his arms hooked around me, he glared at Fear. "Bloody hell, what he is trying to do is just not possible."

"What exactly is he trying to do?"

"He plans to merge with Grim and Fear both," he answered with his lip stuck upward in disgust.

I stared at him in disbelief. "He can't do that, can he?" I asked hopeful. When he didn't answer, my stomach twisted. "I mean, of course he can't," I added. "You and Grim are one, right?"

"I didn't think it was possible for anyone to find a way to separate a merge but he did," Killian replied as his eyebrows pinched together.

Grim was bound by the bright white chain and struggled under its hold. I thought I saw worry flash in Killian's eyes as he looked at Grim, but it quickly turned to resolve. His jaw tightened. "Can you stand?" he spoke softly to me despite the scary gleam in his eyes. He was angry and broken yet he was still checking on me. I nodded and he released me from his hold so that I could stand on my own.

"Go and hide until this is all over," he ordered with a firm and commanding voice. I listened to him.

My eyes followed Killian as he bent down and pulled out a small knife from his boot. My heart crushed. How did he plan to do anything with something so small? Killian wasn't as strong by himself as he was with Grim, was he? My stomach lurched as images raced through my mind. Horrible thoughts. Of me watching Killian die and me being stuck here until I died. I blinked the thoughts away.

No, somehow we were going to make it. He would find a way.

"We were meant to be one." Fear stepped closer to Grim now that the circle around him was gone. Grim wasn't fighting against the chain as Fear spoke. "Merge with me." His arms stretched out wide. He smiled down at Grim, eager and excited. Fear was distracted and Killian snuck up on him. He was behind Fear now, knife aimed above Fear's head—between the horns. I watched hopeful, but that was crushed as I watched Fear's tail dart up like a snake and tear into Killian's chest.

Killian cried out and I found myself crying out with him as I ran to him. I knew he told me to hide somewhere but I couldn't. Killian fell to his knees when Fear brought his tail back out. He moaned, wracked with pain. Blood squirted everywhere now that Fear's tail was out of the hole it tore in his chest. Then the tail swung out again and smacked into Killian's side. He flew several feet off his knees before smacking the ground again and tumbling a few times. I ran faster.

"Foolish." Fear smirked. "You thought to attack me when you are nothing but a weak demon again, Killian," Fear scolded him. "Now, where were we?" He turned back to Grim.

I dropped on the floor next to him and gently grabbed his head, placing it in my lap. His eyes were closed, pinched with pain. I studied his chest. I couldn't see it rising and falling. I sighed in relief when he took in a deep breath, but he started choking and spitting out blood. Blood wasn't good. "Killian, oh God, you're hurt really bad," I whimpered, afraid. I looked at the huge hole in his chest and immediately looked away.

He coughed again as he tried to get up. I held him down. "Your chest." I warned him. He ignored me. And with strength I couldn't imagine from someone who looked on the verge of dying, he pushed my hands away and stood. "Protect you," he whispered hoarsely. He could barely talk. I stood up with him and he leaned into me when I did. "I got to..." His head dropped. "Grim," he muttered before he went completely slack against me. The full brunt of his weight pressed against me. He had to be over two hundred pounds at least, as tall and broad as he was. I tried to push against his weight, but I wasn't strong enough. My grip on his shirt slipped as I fell to the ground with him.

I heard a wailing sound and realized it was me. I maneuvered my body out from underneath him and bent my head over his. Something broke in me. I pressed our foreheads together and touched my hand to his chest. "Killian," I whispered a cry. His heartbeat was faint.

Something erupted and snapped. My head

shot up to see Grim was breaking the chain around him. It popped and snapped, disappearing some more every time he broke the barrier. His essence flared around him again—glowing bright blue before going black. The black essence was his anger, his pain, his revenge. With a hiss, Grim broke the last piece of the chain. It disappeared into nothing like the rest of the chain had.

Grim stood and flexed his arms before he stalked forward. I never thought I would see Fear frightened, but I saw it in his eyes now. The shock and uncertainty in his eyes. Grim seemed to gain more power with every step he took. "Death. I can taste it in the air around you." Grim's voice had changed, the way it did every time he went into Reaper mode. But this time was different. It was more thundering and earth shattering to be heard and witnessed. I released Killian and sat back. It was scary seeing Grim that way. More than he normally was.

"You can't kill me," Fear snapped, but I didn't

miss the waver in his voice.

"You're afraid, Marcus. Can you smell the stench of your own death hanging in the air around you?" Grim's voice raced around the cave walls.

Grim moved fast. He was in Fear's face a second later. He was no match for Grim when he was like that. Grim cupped his skeletal fingers around Fear's neck and he gasped for air. I could see Grim tightening his hold on his neck. Fear's tail shot out in front of him. I panicked and had to look away. I looked back to see that Grim caught his tail with his free hand. Fear clawed at Grim's hand against his neck.

Grim twisted Fear's own tail against him and pointed it to his chest. Fear looked scared, but then he glared. "Your death is coming. I can feel it upon you." He pierced him in the chest with his tail. Fear howled in pain. "But it's not today." He released Fear's neck and dropped him to the ground. When Fear fell the cave walls began to buckle and crumble. Fear was on his knees—one palm against the ground as he gasped for air. The cave was going to bury us inside. I wondered if it had something to do with Fear being injured.

I froze when Grim turned to me. When he started toward me it felt like I was suddenly becoming his prey. I swallowed hard and tried not to let my fear be known. I looked down at Killian. I noticed I was clutching his shirt and my knuckles had gone white. *He can see it,* I thought. He could tell I was afraid of him.

I could tell he was tense as he prowled closer. The echo of his boots seemed to 'thump' in my head louder than the cave crumbling around us. His boots, his clothes, everything was the same as Killian. But he was different. I felt different about him than I did Killian.

He stopped in front of me. His skeletal hands shot out. He grabbed my hand and jerked me to my feet. I ignored the pain I felt every time I moved my body. All my injuries seemed to flare to life letting me know they were there.

He pressed my body into his bones. I stared up in horror. The blue around him was finally back around him, but when he saw the look in my eyes the black came raging back. He grabbed my hand. I realized when it was too late what he was doing. I turned to reach for Killian, but we left him there.

The dark hit me full force, slipping through time and space, into more lights. Then the next thing I knew I was being tossed onto my bed. I looked around my peaceful, quiet room. It felt like a stranger's room.

I looked to Grim standing before me. He wasn't broad like Killian because he was a skeleton yet... he still managed to make the room feel small exactly the way Killian had.

"What about Killian?" I asked immediately

He didn't answer me. He just stood there looking at me with that eyeless face of his. No skin. No flesh. Just a skeleton. I felt nothing. Fear's words nagged in the back of my head.

She could never love you.

As if he could tell what I was thinking—he turned and within a blink. He was gone.

My chest ached. I grabbed it as I staggered to my mirror.

I saw a girl in a white bloodied dress, ripped open in the chest area, exposing the nasty claw marks against her breasts. She was bruised and cut in so many places.

That girl looked wild and scared.

Weak and foolish.

She didn't know anything. Yet...

She survived.

Yes, I was alive. I didn't smile, though. A voice in the back of my head tugged to the surface.

But, are you really?

CHAPTER EIGHTEEN

-Molly-

I appeared in the hospital after leaving Fear. I let the smile creep its way onto my face. When I had been called back to his side, I hadn't expected him to be the *loser.* I took pleasure in seeing the entity injured and hurt. Although it wouldn't last long.

And, he was furious. Fear was a force to be reckoned with. He always thought out every single one of his plans. If one of those fell through, no fuss, he had plenty of more.

Devious bastard.

I grumbled as I walked through the hospital, out of sight, out of mind. I walked through all the doors in the hospital instead of opening them. I couldn't open them even if I wanted to.

Which sucked, but I knew of a lot more stuff that sucked worse. Namely, being a ghost. Also, dying as a young girl and being stuck in that body for three decades.

I stared down at my rag doll dress, the same it had always been since I died. Blood covered a huge chunk of it. How nice would it be to change into some new clothes? I sighed, dreamily. I stared down at my flat chest and short height. I was forever stuck in that state. The state I died in. How nice would it be in I had boobs? And maybe a bit of curves to go with it. I wasn't asking for much, as long as I could get some.

Ah, a ghost could dream.

A pretty young nurse walked right through me as I walked the hall. I tipped my head back and glared at her before running to her and slapping the papers out of her hand. The papers fell around her feet and she bent down to pick them all up. "I'm such a klutz," she groaned and I grinned.

Ah, don't judge me. What was a ghost to do, if not mess with the living? I twirled back around in the direction I was heading and ran through the halls, humming, pretending to be the young girl that I looked. I even held my dress up as I ran.

Because I was Molly. Molly, the dead girl.

I stopped short, dropping my dress down when I reached the room I was supposed to. I passed through the door into a dark room. A boy, well I wouldn't call him that. A young man, broken down and sickly looking lay on the hospital bed.

I sighed and walked next to the bed. *Don't think about it,* I told myself. Most of the time, I did the job and never thought to question the things I did. I met demons when I was a decade old ghost and discovered there were a lot more than ghosts hiding beneath the surface. I also learned I could become something more than just a ghost girl.

I could leave this body of a child and finally become a woman. Something I was denied as a

ghost. Fear had promised me just that if I
continued to do as he asked. I was his right-hand
man—ghost. I just have to do all his dirty work to
get what I wanted. And that is to become a woman.
When that happened, I would also have feeling
again in my body. I would know what warmth felt
like again. I would feel the coldness of each
winter. I would feel the sunshine against my face. I
would eat again and remember what ice cream
used to taste like. I had forgotten what everything
felt like. But, I just had to do what I was told and I
would have it all again.

Normally, I didn't care. Normally...

I just did what I had to without letting
myself think about it. But there were *moments*, rare
ones, like right now when my guilty conscious
slipped through. When that happened, the
hardened soul I made myself become, flickered
and some of the goodness peeked out.

Stupid goodness.

I took another look at the young man. Some

sort of tube ran out of his neck and I wondered if maybe if I just left him alone, let him be, he might just die on his own? As soon as the thought crossed my mind, I swatted it away. No, Fear wouldn't have sent me here if the boy was already dying. The boy was meant to live.

I despised the thought of taking the life of humans. I never had before. First, there was the human girl Melanie. I never succeeded, but if Grim hadn't kept interfering, I knew I would have. I felt the pinch in my chest and ignored it.

Now it was her friend. What was his name? I tried to think of his name. No, it was probably best I didn't know. I was here to kill him anyway.

I stared at his palm and saw Fear's mark. Stupid boy. He got caught up in the girl's problems and now because of it, he would be a bigger part of Fear's plan.

What would Fear do with the boy once he owned his soul, I pondered. It wasn't my job to know. I sighed and climbed the bed until I sat on his chest. I wanted to get this over with before the nagging in my chest tore me to pieces. I knew what I was doing was wrong.

Wrong. Wrong. Wrong.

Sometimes the urge to run from everything and never look back would hit me. Then I would remember I could never go back to just being a ghost. I missed my chance to move on. I couldn't now, not after everything I've done. I was sick thinking about it. I would never know what it was like to walk into Heaven's gates. I would only be sent down to Satan's flames where I'd know nothing but pain and agony.

Okay, enough with thoughts in my head. I pulled the magic knife out of my dress that I kept in the side of my panties. The knife would leave no trace behind. It would look like he died of his injuries instead of what I was about to do.

I brought the knife over my head. It was that moment the young man opened his eyes. I stood there, frozen, forgetting that I was a ghost and he couldn't see me. His eyes scanned the hospital room, in shock and fear, as if he were only realizing now that he was in the hospital. My chest tightened. I closed my eyes.

I sunk the knife into his chest.

Melanie's Story Continues In...

'TIL

GRIM'S

LIGHT

Available Now!

Author's Note

Thank you for reading 'Til Death Do Us Part. I hope you liked it and of course I'd love for you to leave a review. I love to read feedback and as an author I am always wanting to improve.

Now a little about myself... Hmm.

I'm a mom to twin girls who love to keep me busy. When I'm not playing, feeding, and chasing after them or picking up after their father, I try to get some writing in.

I enjoy adventures—in and out of books, reading, watching my favorite TV shows. I might have a slight obsession with Korean dramas and their men. Maybe, it's more than a slight obsession if you were to ask my family and friends, but that's okay. They still love me.

'Til Death Do Us Part is my first published novel, and although it's not perfect, I hope a few of you enjoyed it. Book two is right around the corner.

If you'd like to get in touch or stayed updated on when my next book will be out, feel free to on Facebook:

https://www.facebook.com/michellegrossauthor/

Twitter: @AuthorMichelleG

Instagram: @michellegrossmg

Join my mailing list at:

http://eepurl.com/cRXrUX